CHRISTMAS WISHES
&
POPCORN KISSES

Christmas Wishes
&
Popcorn Kisses

A festive romantic comedy

CHLOË L BLYTH

For all who have ever wondered,
"What if Father Christmas was hot?"

And all who haven't.

Glossary

Nibling(n) –
A child of your sibling.

Father Christmas(n) –
What us British folk call 'Santa.'

Hangry(adj) –
Bad-tempered or irritable as a result of hunger.

1

Hi, my name is Abi, and I am a fraud. Not the kind who steals identities or money, the kind who smiles and says everything is fine when in reality, everything is falling apart.

Six weeks ago, I split up with my boyfriend and started renting the first place I could find. There's a spider in every corner of every room, the windows sort of rattle, and there's a stagnant smoke smell despite the no-smoking policy. And the bathroom... yikes. It's like something out of the 70s. Well, not *like*. It *is*, probably. It looks original. You certainly can't buy that kind of thing in IKEA.

To top it all off, I'm being made redundant. So, this Christmas is looking really flipping merry and January doesn't even bear thinking about. There are only so many jobs you can apply for before the rejections become a bit too much, especially so soon after being dumped. I've never felt so alone.

That's partly why I'm getting my nails done, to socialise. I listen to Siobhan's plans for an exciting Christmas and New Year's Eve abroad with her absolute hunk of a boyfriend, whom she believes might pop the question, as she shapes and buffs my nails before applying my signature colour. I recently had my acrylics removed and I can't stand how short and stubby my nails look, but I just can't afford the maintenance right now. The plan was to start doing my nails myself, but I couldn't resist one final treat before I start living within my means. Life was so much cheaper when the bills were split between two.

As she applies the topcoat, my phone starts ringing in my bag.

"Do you want me to help you get that?" Siobhan offers, and I accept. She unzips my bag and places my phone on the table so I can see the screen and carefully tap it without ruining my nails. It's my sister, Charlotte. I answer on speakerphone.

"Hey Char, can I call you back? I'm just at the salon," I tell her quickly, not wanting anyone to overhear our usual sisterly conversations which are definitely not suitable for public ears. Any topic is up for discussion between the two of us as I am her older sister, friend, and number one confidante.

"Abi, Mike's gone! I need you!" she sounds whiney, like she's crying. I look up at Siobhan and she lets go of my left pinkie finger. I tap my phone to turn off the speakerphone and hold it carefully to my ear with my fingers splayed out to avoid getting any hair stuck to the wet polish. I stand and move towards the window, talking quietly.

"What do you mean, he's gone?"

"He's gone! He's not here. I don't know where he is! We had an argument last night and I woke up this morning and he wasn't there! At first I thought, maybe he went for a bike ride, but his bike is still here. His car's gone, and he's not answering his phone. Abi, I don't know what to do! I can't do this on my own, I can't!" I hear a crash like tumbling plastic in the background followed by the high-pitched wail of a young child. "Abi, please help me! I know you don't need to work right now, so why don't you use up those final days' leave you're owed and come and look after the kids whilst I go find their daddy? I need you. Please. Abi? Abi, say something, please. Abi?"

I stare outside at the families rushing past the window with kids wrapped in thick warm coats that are so big they look as if they would bounce if they fell over. They clasp their parents' hands with joy and skip along. Could I look after a thirteen-month-old and a four-year-old, with no experience?

"Char, I don't know. I've never looked after them on my own before…"

"You'll be fine, you're their auntie. And I have a whole bunch of activities planned, so you can just work your way through those, and then I'll be back before you know it," she sniffs. Today is the fifteenth of December. Even I know this is the time of year that kids are at their most energetic, positively bursting with excitement. Jasmine might be too young to really understand, but Nero is going to be a nightmare.

"But what about poo time, nappy changes, and Nero – does he wipe himself yet?" I ask, lowering my voice even more.

"You'll be fine. If I can do it, so can you!" she chirps with fake enthusiasm. I sigh. That is so not true, but it's not worth arguing about. "So, what time can you get here? I've had a look and there's a train leaving London St Pancreas at 6pm, so I can be in Paris by-"

"-Paris?" I interrupt her. "You're leaving the country? What if I need you? What if the kids get sick or have an accident?"

"You'll be fine. It's a long story, I'll explain when you get here… if there's time. So, you'll be on your way then? If you forget to pack anything, just help yourself to my stuff.

3

Okay?" she already sounds brighter even though I don't recall agreeing to anything yet. She knows I never say 'no' to her.

"I'll be there."

I return to the table where Siobhan is waiting for me.

"Well, it sounds like your Christmas just got a lot more interesting, huh? It's not quite the trip to Iceland that I'm going on, but I'm sure it'll be lovely, spending time with your niece and nephew," she smiles. How did she overhear all of that? I nod,

"Uhuh, yup. I'm sure it's going to be great. Probably for the best that I don't have my long nails anymore, hey?" I joke, picking up my handbag. I paid when I booked, so I'm free to leave.

"See you in the new year?" she asks.

"Hopefully," I reply with a grimace. If I don't find a new job, there's no way I'll be paying to have my nails done again. I'll probably get kicked out of my flat and end up moving in with Charlotte permanently as a live-in Nanny. Lord, help me!

2

Packing my bags is quick and easy because I never fully unpacked. I like to believe that my boxes and bags offer an extra layer of protection against spiders nesting amongst my belongings, and I can't quite bring myself to unpack my clothes into the built-in wardrobe due to my irrational fear that I will one day open the aforementioned wardrobe and find a cobweb so thick it belongs in the film 'Arachnophobia.' What if a spider traps me in there and wraps me up like a fly? It's not like there's anyone around to save me before I get eaten. My body might never be found!

The flat is bitterly cold thanks to the drafty windows and useless 80s style electric storage heaters, so I have to keep moving and rubbing my hands together to stave off frostbite. Honestly, I would never have chosen to live here if I hadn't been so desperate to move quickly. This place was vacant, unsurprisingly, so I only had to crash at a friend's house until the paperwork was sorted. I couldn't bear to go back to the apartment I'd shared with Toby; I didn't want to see his face again. Correction: I never want to see his face again.

When I'm shivering alone at night, I often turn to wine to keep me warm. Only out of necessity, I assure you. It has nothing to do with being broken-hearted, it's simply cheaper than paying for heating that doesn't work. I have blankets and pinot grigio – or whatever is on offer at the local shop – and it works perfectly. I am going to enjoy having quality gas central heating at Charlotte's though, I might even bring my short pyjamas!

Fortunately for Charlotte, I didn't drink last night, so I am perfectly safe to drive to her house a little over two hours away. I chuck my bags into my car boot, make a quick stop for fuel – just the right amount, I hope, as I don't want to pay to fill the tank – and start my journey.

As I drive, my brain tries to process everything that's happened in the past hour. I think I'm still in shock. I will always do anything to help my little sister, and she knows that, but I have so many questions and I can't really believe she has asked me to look after her children. *Me.* The woman with no experience whatsoever. I don't *do* kids. Playgroups and story-time and well, whatever else is involved are completely foreign to me. I don't even watch programmes with kids in. (They don't tend to feature in reality tv dating shows, which are almost exclusively the only programmes I watch).

When I first moved in and set up my rubbish TV which I have been carting around with me since university (because of course Toby claimed the big, fancy one we bought together), I binged an entire series of '*Love Under The Stars,*' and it was fabulous. Somehow losing myself in other people's romantic drama was just what I needed. And the guys were nice to look at, too. There was this one guy, Jacob… Oh boy would I have crawled into his tent!

As I merge onto the motorway, I wonder what I'm going to be stuck watching for the next few days. Are the

Teletubbies still a thing? Bill and Ben, the Flowerpot Men? Probably not. And I'm guessing Bananas in Pyjamas are long gone; the more I think about that theme song, the more I'm thinking some adults were really having a laugh with that one and our innocent minds had no idea. *Bananas in pyjamas, are coming down the stairs…* yeesh.

Unless it's my mind that's the problem? A side-effect from seeing too many 'bananas' in pyjamas?

I turn up the radio. If I had a more modern car, with Bluetooth, I'd connect my phone and call Charlotte to run through all these questions on the way. Instead, it's me, the radio, and my overactive mind.

The radio does nothing to quiet my thoughts, so I turn it down and analyse. Mike and Charlotte have always seemed like a strong couple. Both homebodies, both wanted kids, both happy living their simple life. It's not my cup of tea, but it has always seemed right for them. I can't believe he would have run away. There's got to be more to it.

Could Charlotte have cheated on Mike? We've joked before about their chatty postman, but she wouldn't have actually done something, would she?

And why Paris? As far as I know, Mike has no connection to Paris whatsoever. He grew up in Kent and all his family are over here. I should know, I met them all at their wedding. I got to know his weird cousins Anthony and Barney particularly well as we were all dumped on the Singles Table thanks to my boyfriend of the time ditching me two weeks prior.

Oh yeah, didn't I mention this isn't the first time I've been dumped or cheated on? I'm sure it won't be the last either. Not that I mind, it's the beginning of a relationship that's the fun part anyway.

And, if you believe that, you're more gullible than I am. But anyway, like I told you at the start, I'm a fraud and if anyone asks, I will always say I'M FINE. Because I am. Okay?

The roads start to look more familiar as I come off the motorway and head towards the town we grew up in. Charlotte never moved away. Me, I was off to the big city, lured by hot yoga and Singles' Salsa Nights. And bars, so many bars. I never wanted to settle down and do the whole marriage and babies thing, but it might have been nice to have the choice. A willing accomplice. Someone who wasn't out to shatter my heart yet again.

3

As I enter the house, I immediately notice the packed suitcase waiting just inside the door. I can hear a Christmas movie playing, somebody crying, and, as I follow Charlotte through to the lounge, I am faced with a bare Christmas tree in dire need of decorations and, even worse, a small bare bottom headed this way. My eyes open wide in alarm as Nero walks butt-first towards us, screaming "Mummy!"

Charlotte looks at me and smiles,

"Oh, you'll get used to that. Come on Nero, back to the bathroom, I'll wipe you. Abi, do you want to come and watch how it's done?" Talk about diving in headfirst.

"Um, no, I think we'll figure it out..." I say, looking for somewhere to put my bags down and trying to remove the image from my mind.

The lounge is full of clutter: toys, rubbish, food crumbs and plastic beakers. I guess Charlotte usually tidies up before I get here. Next to the undressed Christmas tree is a box of decorations and a giant knot of fairy lights, so I'm guessing that's my first job. Great. I hate untangling Christmas lights. I didn't even put lights on my tree last year, I hate it that much. I had a dull tinsel and bauble tree which looked okay

9

in daytime and completely miserable at night. A bit like me, I suppose. Though back then I was in blissful ignorance about what Toby was up to as I waited for him to get home, later and later... Oh boy do I need a drink.

I push thoughts of Toby from my mind and put my bags on the floor, then try to clear a space to sit on the sofa.

Charlotte re-enters the room holding a plastic wallet filled with A4 paper just as I pull a toy dinosaur out from behind a cushion. I place it on the floor where it can no longer jab me in the back.

"I've written down everything I could think of. Bedtimes, food likes and dislikes – luckily no allergies – your itinerary, including meeting Father Christmas," she looks at me to emphasise the importance of this, "and what to leave out on Christmas Eve if I'm running late."

I frown at her.

"But you're going to be back well before then, aren't you? That's nine days away! I can't host Christmas on my own!"

"I'm just covering all eventualities; I'm sure we'll both be back in a couple of days." Her smile doesn't quite reach her eyes.

"Are you okay Char? Is there anything more you can tell me now that I'm here?" She shrugs noncommittally, watching Nero as he plays carefully with his little sister, Jasmine. I continue. "Were you having problems? Did you… do something?"

"No!" she says a little too quickly. "We were fine, we *are* fine. We just had one little argument and then he disappeared!"

"Daddy gone!" Nero echoes, clearly paying more attention than I thought.

"And why do you think he's gone to Paris?" I ask more quietly.

"It doesn't matter," she sighs. "Look, if you need me, I'll have my phone. I really need to get going…" she lifts her left wrist exaggeratedly to get her Fitbit to light up and show the time.

"Seriously? You're not going to give me anything more than that? After I came all this way to look after your kids for you?"

"I really appreciate it, but I just can't, okay? I can't talk about it. I need to find him. I need to get him back in time for Christmas. Thank you, Abi. Nero, you be good for Auntie Abi, alright? Father Christmas is watching. And you too, Jasmine!" she kneels and cuddles and kisses them both before standing up and looking at me once more. "Thank you, sis. I owe you one."

There are tears in her eyes.

4

She owes me more than bloody one. It's only been three days and already I feel like a prisoner of war, trapped and under the control of two small children who miss their parents. I am not cut out for this. I have matted hair, I do not know what is stuck in it, but I do know it is the kind of knotted mess you cut out of a dog's fur. It's bad. I haven't managed to shower since I arrived because every time I go into the bathroom, Jasmine cries or Nero asks me for something. I am exhausted, and dirty.

The poo situation? Well, every time 'shit happens,' it's a miracle any of us survive. Nero still likes to surprise me, bum first, in any room of the house, and I have a newfound sympathy for my mum. She was never a keen bum-wiper and when she did it, it hurt. That's all I remember, it hurt. I've been trying my best not to repeat history by hurting Nero when he bends forward in front of the toilet, but he still cries out in pain as if it's my fault his poo won't come away from his skin without a bit of force. The boy should be glad I had my acrylic nails removed before I came here. It could have been much worse, for both of us.

12

Coffee is the only thing keeping me going, but there's no chance of getting another caffeine fix until after we've met Father Christmas. We're currently queuing in the local shopping centre as per Charlotte's itinerary, to do just that. There's Christmas music playing, children squealing and crying at ear-damaging frequencies, decorations everywhere, and a hunger-inducing scent of gingerbread. I'm sure that's being pumped in on purpose to ensure that everyone who waits their turn in line goes straight to the café once they've seen the guy in red.

Nero's hand is hot and sticky with excitement and he keeps yanking my arm to go look at toys, but I am not letting go. This is my job now; I cannot fail my sister. Could you imagine if I lost her son? Jasmine, on the other hand, is fast asleep. That little darling could sleep in a nightclub.

We shuffle forward in the queue. I am proud of my nephew for being so patient, but I suppose that's only because of who we're here to see and all of that 'Naughty or Nice' list nonsense. He would probably be a nightmare if he knew his mother's wardrobe was already crammed full of presents for him and his sister, and that he's going to get them whether he behaves or not. Well, so long as I find them all. If it comes to that. But Charlotte will be back in time for Christmas, won't she? She wouldn't leave her kids with Auntie Abi on the most important day of the year for them, would she? She wouldn't give them a Christmas with no parents, just because Mike went AWOL, right?

I pull out my phone from my bag which is securely attached to the pushchair – it really is quite a handy transport device to push around, it's giving my shoulders a nice rest – and tap out a quick message to Charlotte.

Just in the queue to see Father C, any sign of M yet? Xx

I consider sending her a photo of Nero as he holds onto the pushchair and beams up at me like butter wouldn't melt, but ultimately decide against it. She's busy. I still take the photo though, because he is looking annoyingly adorable right now and I suppose it is good for me to record this time away from my normal life. I usually only take photos of my dinner, or a nice-looking cocktail on a night out. I'm sorry to admit I am one of 'those' people. My Instagram account is basically an advert for all the food and drink venues in my local area, and yet, I'm still not an influencer, and I still have to pay for my cocktails on Girls' Night. Which reminds me, I'm missing our Christmas drinks this weekend – we normally go heavy on the mulled wine with rum. I'll have to tell Stacie to have one for me.

As we creep forwards, we discuss what we think Father Christmas is going to smell like. I keep my true thoughts to myself like a good Auntie and suggest candyfloss, gingerbread, or tinsel. This makes Nero laugh because he doesn't believe me that tinsel has a smell.

I really hope this Father Christmas is a good one, at least not a heavy smoker, or fuelled by alcohol, because I strongly suspect Nero is going to give him a good sniff. They do background checks these days, right?

Turning the corner, I finally get a look at Father Christmas' Helpers, and I am pleasantly surprised. The 'elves' are clearly local students, drama students if I had to guess, and they are very enthusiastic and well presented. The costumes are on point, and I'm not referring to their ears. This gives me hope that whoever selected them also selected a good, safe, Father Christmas. A kind old man, perhaps with a genuine big belly or white beard. Maybe a local drama teacher. Just not a paedophile, please not a paedophile.

When I said I watch reality TV, that includes crime documentaries, and Father Christmas is the creepiest potential criminal I've come across. He is literally a walking disguise and child magnet; the possibilities are horrendous. Thank goodness we don't place children in their laps anymore.

We don't, right? They get to sit in a tiny chair beside him, don't they? My nephew had better get a tiny chair!

Nero twists around, taking in all the new scenery and pointing at the helpers. He's gone a bit shy though and refuses to talk to them when they ask him his name and if he's been a good boy. I tell them that he's been a very good boy and accept a candy cane on his behalf. I'm not sure if he's allowed it, but Auntie Abi can take care of it if not.

My evening wine has been replaced by sugary treats whilst I'm here anyway, I'm too afraid to drink. What if something happens to Jasmine or Nero and they need me to take them to the hospital, but I've been drinking so I can't, and we have to wait for a taxi, or an ambulance, and it takes too long, and something awful happens? I don't know how parents ever drink. I think I'd have to do 18 years of sobriety, or 21 to get through those clubbing years too. Thank God this is only temporary.

I squeeze Nero's hand and bend down to talk to him,

"Do you know what you're going to say to Father Christmas?" He nods his head enthusiastically.

"I'm good boy and I want sca-ticks. Peas!" I recently deciphered that sca-ticks means Scalextric, those racing cars on the tracks which you control with a remote. Mike is into Formula One, so Nero has inherited his interest in fast cars.

"That's right! And when he gives you a present, what do you say?"

"Fank you!" Maybe this parenting stuff isn't so bad.

We curve around the path following the queue and are now only a few from the front. I still can't see Father Christmas though; he is deliberately hidden in his 'grotto' so that you can only see him when it's your turn.

My nose becomes aware of a scent that has started to become increasingly familiar. Jasmine. But not *Jasmine* Jasmine, Jasmine as in Jasmine has done a stinker in her nappy and is about to start crying. Not now, oh please not now! I reach into my handbag and try to discreetly spray a few bursts of perfume to cover up the smell. We only need to get through the 'meet Father Christmas' business and then we can go to the baby-change. I am not leaving the queue now.

"Auntie," Nero pulls my arm.

"Yes sweetie," I answer.

"Smean smells," he says, holding his nose with his other hand.

"Yes, I know," I tell him, lowering my voice, "but we can't change her until after you've seen Father Christmas. Otherwise, we'll have to go back to the end of the queue. You don't want to wait that long, do you?"

He shakes his head.

"Okay, so just hold your nose and we'll clean her up as soon as you've told Father Christmas what you would like for Christmas."

Jasmine chooses that moment to start crying at full volume. I hurry to the front of the pushchair to release her into my arms. Oh man, she stinks. I've made the smell so much worse by releasing her from her chair!

She's howling now as I bounce her and rub her back and stare hopelessly into her pink face. I don't know what I'm doing. A busybody mother from behind informs me that, "perhaps she needs changing." *No shit, Sherlock.* Or rather, lots of shit, Sherlock. I "mm" noncommittally because I am not losing our space in this queue, we're next.

The elf in charge of letting the children through to see Father Christmas looks at us nervously.

"Are all three of you going through to see Father Christmas?" she asks over Jasmine's cries.

"Well, Nero wants to see him properly; we'll just watch," I try to explain. Nero holds my hand tighter.

"You're not coming with me?" he asks.

"I can't sweetie, I've got to look after your sister. I'll watch from the doorway." I try to reassure him. His eyes well up.

"I'm sorry, we can't let anyone watch from the doorway, you will have to wait outside if you're not going in," the elf informs us.

"Then we're all going in," I tell her.

"Yeah, it's just that we don't normally let crying babies inside…" she bites her lip nervously.

"So, you're suggesting that I let this little boy go in and meet a stranger on his own?" I ask, incredulous. She nods,

"It's quite safe."

"Do you have any children, elf? How well do you know Father Christmas? Would you leave your child with a stranger?"

"No, I, er, I met him this season, and erm, well, if she's crying… it's, um, I'm so sorry…" I realise I have upset this teenager with my bolshy new mum-itude. Jasmine continues to wriggle and scream in my arms, so I raise my voice,

17

"I am not letting this boy go in there on his own!"

"Yes, of course, err," she looks at her supervisor who is making her way towards us.

"Can we discuss this somewhere quieter, perhaps?" the supervisor asks, her face unable to hide her disgust of 'le parfum de Jasmine.'

"That won't be necessary, we're at the front now. We will just pop in and see Father Christmas quickly, and then we'll be out of your hair. Isn't that right, Nero?" I look down at the little boy who seems rather afraid of all the drama. He nods.

The two women exchange a look.

"Santa isn't good with babies," the supervisor informs me quietly.

"Seriously? Whose idea was it to hire him? I'm not going to dump the baby in his lap, we'll just stand in the corner whilst Nero does his bit and then we'll be gone."

"I'm not sure that's going to work, with the smell… he's quite demanding, you see."

"And again, whose idea was it to hire a demanding man who doesn't like babies and can't deal with a little bit of poo smell to be Father Christmas? Who is this guy? He must be pretty bloody perfect to have made all these demands. Real beard is it? Real fat belly?" I poke at my own slim stomach with unintentional force and try not to wince.

The supervisor's eyes flash with concern, but it's fine, Nero knows this isn't the real Father Christmas. He knows Father Christmas can't be in every shopping centre at the same time, he knows people are hired to pass on the messages. It doesn't stop him thinking they're special though. Magic, and whatever.

"You don't know, do you?" the original elf asks.

"Don't know what?"

"Who he is! The reason our queue is the longest it's ever been! This is not just your average Mr Claus!" The elf beams with excitement, clearly no longer afraid of me, the fool who doesn't know who Father Christmas is. "It's Jacob Chilbeam from '*Love Under The Stars*,' you know, the dating show? He's not a fat Santa, he's a hot Santa!"

I don't even pause to let that sink in.

"Excuse me? You're telling me that we queued to meet Father Christmas, and he's *not* a fat old man with a white beard?"

"Oh no, he is, he's wearing the usual stuff, but you know... he's not, underneath." The girl blushes. Right. In another frame of mind, I would also be blushing and thinking about him topless by a campfire, but not now. Now, my mum-itude is in full swing and I am furious.

"Well, we want to see a Father Christmas who looks like a Father Christmas, don't we Nero?" I look down, hoping he'll agree. Before he can answer, the door into the 'grotto' is opened and Father Christmas himself makes a brief appearance.

Damn, they weren't kidding. I might only be able to see his eyes and nose, but that man is sex on a stick, as they say... when they're not looking after their sister's children. He has a sparkle in his eye, and such a good nose. He even makes those red trousers look good. It must be the way his muscular thighs fill them...

"What's the hold up?" he asks, snapping me out of my daydream. "And what is that smell?" He wrinkles his nose and glares at Jasmine like she's a big sack of screaming rubbish.

"This woman would like to bring the baby in with her too," the supervisor explains.

"Nah, not gonna happen. Move along, I've got to get through ten more visits before I can have a break and I'm dying for a piss." He closes the door. Jerk.

"Why is Father Kissmas angry?" Nero asks with a sad face.

"Don't worry, that was Father Christmas' son, but he wasn't very nice. Let's go clean up Jasmine and then we can find somewhere else to see Father Christmas."

"But I want to see him now!" Nero shouts and stamps his foot. Great, that's all I need, a tantrum on top of the screaming poo baby. The glares are coming at us from all angles now.

"I know, but that Father Christmas won't see Jasmine, so we're going to have to go somewhere else."

"Don't care Smean, I want sca-ticks!"

"Do you want to go in there on your own to see him?" I ask, believing the TV star who hates kids is unlikely to be a child-molester. Nero shakes his head.

I clip Jasmine back into the pushchair, and we walk back up the queue, stinking everyone out as we go.

5

The baby-change is in use, of course, so we join yet another queue. Is this what it's like to have children? Constant queueing?

By the time Jasmine is clean and fed and not crying, Nero and I are hangry, really hangry. Chocolate flavoured children's cereal just doesn't fill me up the way it used to when I was five. Nero is already whimpering and I'm about ready to burst into tears myself when we finally reach the food counter to purchase some overpriced cheese sandwiches, because I'm not used to packing a picnic like the clever mums, when who should dare to step in front of us? To cut into the queue like the most important person in the shopping centre? Oh, you guessed it alright.

He's not wearing his red outfit anymore, but I can tell it's him by his total lack of manners and air of self-importance. The guy has a job dressing up as Father Christmas, doesn't he realise that's the bottom of the ladder, not the top? Most people who come out of TV shows end up on other TV shows or maybe they get modelling contracts, especially people who look like him... The fact he's playing dress up should make him feel rubbish, shouldn't it?

Not that that's what's really bothering me, what's really bothering me is that he cut in front of us, I am starving, and he has just ordered the second to last cheese sandwich which means that I am now going to have to sacrifice the final sandwich to Nero and quiet my own hunger pangs with ready salted crisps and a latte.

In her pushchair, Jasmine blows a raspberry and then giggles as Nero does it back to her. They're so sweet together. Jacob Chilbeam immediately whips his head round to check that nothing has been splattered onto the back of his trousers. His eyes narrow at us.

"Oh, it's you."

I smile politely.

"Auntie Abi, do you know him?" asks Nero.

"No sweetie, I don't. He just jumped the queue and stole my cheese sandwich," I tell him with a straight face.

"Do I still get cheese sandwich?" he frowns with concern.

"Yes sweetie, don't worry, there's one left for you."

"Excuse me?" Jacob Chilbeam asks, seemingly put out by my honesty.

"What?"

"I didn't steal your cheese sandwich; it wasn't yours to steal!"

"Well, it would have been mine if you hadn't jumped the queue like you own the place!" I tell him as he taps his card and moves to the side to wait for his drink. They didn't show that side of him on the TV. I should have known that no one who looks like him can have a good personality too, it's too much for one guy. It wouldn't be fair.

I order the cheese sandwich for Nero, two packets of crisps, my latte, and a carton of juice. The only sandwiches left are tuna salad (which turns my stomach just looking at them), so it's going to be a long hungry afternoon for me.

22

"I'm sorry, you can have it if you want. I'm not meant to be eating cheese anyway," Jacob Chilbeam offers me the sandwich as we move to the side to wait for my latte.

"Oh no, I'm not having your pity sandwich. You wanted it, you got it."

He receives his drink and shrugs.

"Alright then. Sorry about earlier, I get a bit cranky when I'm hungry. You know how it is," he winks at me and then walks away. *Was he suggesting that I'm cranky because I'm hungry, when he's the reason I'm going to remain hungry? The audacity!* I let out a large sigh of annoyance.

"Auntie, when are we going to meet Father Kissmas?" Nero asks once we are seated at a small table with Jasmine awkwardly positioned in her pushchair beside us, blocking the path between tables.

"I'm not sure yet. You eat your sandwich, and I'll have a look."

It's the 18th December, there's got to be loads of opportunities around. Unlocking my phone, I see Charlotte has replied.

Nothing yet. Oh good, I hear he's a Sexy Santa this year! Enjoy! Xx

She knew! Well, she could have bloody warned me, couldn't she? I quickly tap out a response.

Sexy and arrogant. Wouldn't let us in because Jasmine needed changing. Now got to find somewhere else to go.

She replies quickly.

23

Good luck with that, everything's pre-booked this year. You're better off re-joining the queue there. I assume you have changed her now?

Believing that doesn't require an answer, I switch to my internet browser and search for 'meet Father Christmas' in this area. There are all sorts of results from 'breakfast with Santa' to 'photos with Father Christmas' and, most disturbing of all, 'Santa home visit.' I won't bore you with all the reasons that disturbs me. Letting a strange fat man into your house to meet your children? No, no, no, no, no! If I can't find a regular Father Christmas to visit who isn't booked up, Nero will just have to accept that you can't see him every year, or I'll dress up myself. In this day and age, Father Christmas can be a woman with breasts if he wants to be!

"Nero, do you want to try to see Father Christmas' son again, or do you want to go home and make paperchains and watch a Christmas movie?"

"I need to tell him about the sca-ticks!" he sticks out his bottom lip.

"Well, I can tell him for you, if you want. I have his email address."

"Really?" he considers. "No, I want to tell him myself."

"Okay, let's go join the queue again." I push Jasmine into position, ready to navigate our way out of the café and back to the end of the queue, whilst holding on tightly to Nero. I lean forwards over the pushchair and jokingly tell Jasmine, "No poopies this time, okay missy?"

She giggles and wiggles her feet.

"How long is it going to take, Auntie?" asks Nero once we have secured our place at the back of the queue.

"I don't know."

"How long does it take to get to the North Pole?"

"A really long time."

"Have you been there? Is it cold? Is it really snowy?"

"No I haven't, but yes, I believe so."

"So, they can build snowmen all the time? Wow! What do you think Father Kissmas has for breakfast?"

And so the questions go, on and on, until we finally find ourselves outside Father Christmas' grotto once again. Fortunately, it's a different elf on door duty now, so we aren't recognised from earlier.

"Are you all going in?" she asks.

"Yes, we are." I reply with confidence. There are no smelly nappies or tears this time around. We can do this!

We hear a bell ring on the other side, and the elf slowly opens the door, peeks inside, then ushers us in. We follow a glittering path towards where Father Christmas is sat on a large red armchair. There is a small wooden chair beside him.

"Go on then," I tell Nero, patting him softly on the back. He looks nervously at the man wearing the obviously fake white beard.

"You come too," he says, reaching for my hand.

"I need to stay here with Jasmine," I explain, not wanting a repeat of earlier. At least we've made it to the other side of the door this time.

"Peas Auntie, bring Smean too," he begs.

What can I say? I'm a sucker for puppy-dog eyes. I'm not a parent, I'm allowed to be manipulated by my nephew. It's not like it's all the time.

"Alright then, here goes," I say, reaching in to unbuckle Jasmine and then carrying her with me towards the armchair containing a very concerned looking Father Christmas. I guess it's true, he really doesn't like babies. Not that Jasmine feels much like a baby, she's a right wriggler and I'm sure she's going to be walking any day now. She's mastered the bum shuffle at an impressive speed. It was quite a sight to behold, her shuffling on her bum, and Nero shuffling bum up, towards me in my sister's lounge last night. It was like a glimpse of a life I could have had, but bizarrely bum orientated.

I hold her heavy weight and we stand next to a pile of presents. Jasmine stretches and reaches her little fingers towards everything in sight.

Finally, Nero is brave enough to sit next to Father Christmas and he looks at him very seriously.

"My name is Nero, I live at 7 Appletree Road and that's Auntie Abi and my sister Smean. What I want for Kissmas, peas, is sca-ticks and my daddy. Daddy gone missing so Mummy gone to find him, so Auntie come to stay. Peas get something nice for Auntie, too. She had to clean Smean's poopie."

I smile with a tear in my eye. What a sweet, sweet little boy. Father Christmas a.k.a. Jacob Chilbeam catches my eye, and my belly does an involuntary flip. Who am I kidding? He's absolutely my type, selfish or not. And, I might as well admit it, he was my favourite on '*Love Under The Stars.*'

We pose together for a group photo, which is going to cost Auntie far too much, and then Nero clasps his wrapped present tightly in his little hands and carefully looks around it to take the two steps down from the area with the armchair and then waits beside the pushchair.

"Sorry, again, for earlier. I didn't realise. It must be hard taking on your niece and nephew," says Father Christmas. No, Jacob Chilbeam. Jacob. Can I call him Jacob now that we've met three times?

"Don't worry about it, it's been a tough few days, but we're getting through it. This isn't my usual scene either, so I get the whole 'keep babies away from me' thing. It's a smell you never get used to."

"Yeah, well, I could have been more accommodating. If I'd realised you were their auntie, I would've-"

"What?" I cut him off. "It wouldn't have made her poop smell any sweeter."

"No, but you know what I mean. I thought you were some lazy mum who expects the world to put up with the smell of her child's poop because she can't be bothered to re-join the queue."

"Ouch, not helping yourself there; have you seen how long that queue is? And have you heard how often babies poop? Thanks for being, uh, nicer this time, but I hope I don't bump into you again, if you know what I mean. You're best left on TV."

A grin lights up his face.

"Oh, you watched the show?"

"Yep, and I'm going to go now, before we get kicked out for taking too long," I say before making my way back to the pushchair, once I've managed to disentangle Jasmine's fingers from some bizarrely stringy fake snow from the artificial Christmas tree that could almost double as cobweb at Halloween. Maybe it does.

"Wait!"

I turn to look back and he clomps over in his big black boots.

"Give me a call when you're done with babysitting duty, yeah?"

I take the piece of paper from his hand and put it straight in my back pocket ready to be forgotten and go through a wash cycle.

When we finally leave the building and head out towards my sister's giant 'mum car' that I'm currently borrowing, Nero hounds me with more questions.

"What did Father Kissmas' son give you? Are you going to be boyfriend and girlfriend now? I think he likes you. Did you smell him? He smelled like popcorn and cheese!"

6

Popcorn and cheese. After several hours of trying to put Nero to bed, he is finally asleep, as is Jasmine (for now), and I find myself curled up on the sofa in my pyjamas watching the man who smells like popcorn and cheese (a re-run of '*Love Under The Stars*').

I thought I would study his behaviour to see if he seemed as much of a selfish sandwich-stealing poopy-pants (my new favourite and recently acquired insult) on the show as he was today. So far, I've seen a lot of his bum, and not much of anything else. There was fun challenge which involved squeezing his glutes to keep hold of items, and he was very good at it. From the way they portrayed him on the show, I can't believe none of the women picked him at the end. But then again, maybe that's a clue in itself: he can't have been that great or one of them would have. Maybe he kept his sandwich-stealing behaviour behind the scenes, and the women on the show knew more than us viewers. He certainly didn't seem so perfect in real life.

I reach for my phone and call Charlotte again. No answer. She didn't answer when I first started trying to put Nero to bed either. He really wanted to see her and have her sing 'Sleeps 'til Santa' to him because, apparently, I'm rubbish at it and don't do it right. I also don't know all the words yet, but I'm trying my best. It's a steep learning curve when you've never had or lived with little kids since you were one of them.

Urgh, that reminds me, I need to move that bloody elf on the shelf to some other silly place before morning. I know some parents get really creative with their elves, so I don't want to let the side down. I wander into the kitchen holding the mischievous elf.

"What do you want to do Elfie?" I ask it, then study its smug face. Definitely not an Elfie. "Sorry, Elf*ward*, if I'm not allowed rum then neither are you. Hmm… How do you feel about baking?"

I put the elf down on the worktop and position the portable steps so that I'll be able to climb and reach the top shelf of the cupboard where the flour is kept. As I'm standing on the top step, carefully manoeuvring the bag of flour out from between a bag of icing sugar and a carefully positioned line of miniature bottles filled with assorted essences – with vanilla clearly the only one that's been opened – a young voice says "whoa" making me jump out of my skin, drop the bag of flour, and knock several of the miniature bottles onto the floor.

I stare down at the damage: the bottles are fine, the flour exploded everywhere, and Nero is stood with an odd look on his face. That's when I remember that these pyjama bottoms are rather short and airy and that when I was leaning forwards and carefully manoeuvring the flour, from his lower position, he likely had a view of, well… everything. Everything a little boy should never see. Heat rises to my face.

Ignoring the mess on the floor, I adjust my pyjamas and turn to face him.

"Nero, what can I do for you? It's late, you should be asleep."

"I had a bad dream. Will you sing to me?"

"Sing to you?" Charlotte never mentioned singing. There was no list of favourite songs in the stack of papers she gave me, and we both know how badly my attempt at 'Sleeps 'til Santa' has been going.

"Mummy sings to me when I have a bad dream," he explains sadly before squeezing the front of his trousers.

"Do you need the toilet?"

He nods.

"Okay, well how about you go to the toilet whilst I clean this up, and then I'll sing you a song. How does that sound?"

"What were you doing?" he asks, looking at the flour-covered floor. I grab the elf.

"Elfward here was going to do some baking for you, so I was getting the ingredients down for him." Nero giggles.

"Elves can't cook!"

"Well, this one can. But he won't be any more, not now that I've dropped the flour." Nero sticks his bottom lip out.

"I'm sowee. I didn't mean to scare you."

"That's okay, sweetie. Now, you go to the toilet, and I'll be right through to sing you to sleep." I can tell he has something else he wants to say from the way he's frowning at me.

"You have a nice lady-bum Auntie Abi, it's not hairy like Mummy's."

Jesus Christ! I did not need to know that Charlotte had let her pubic hair grow. And Nero didn't need to know that I haven't.

"Erm, thank you?" I say, uncertainly. "But we shouldn't talk about lady-bums, okay? Can we pretend you didn't see mine, Nero?"

He nods and walks away.

31

7

The next evening, booming Christmas music perks Nero up from his post-mince pie strop on the sofa. He wipes his eyes and rushes to open the curtains and look outside. It's Father Christmas, again! One of the local charities always arranges for a lorry to drive around the area with Father Christmas in the run up to Christmas. It stops on every street, pleasing all the children, and is an extra chance to get a photo with the big guy for those who have missed out on seeing him elsewhere. There are many photos of Charlotte and I outside in pyjamas with the Father Christmas of our era, Dad was great at ensuring we never missed it. In fact, the only year we missed it, was the year Mum didn't come home. We didn't really do Christmas that year.

"Can we, can we, can we?" Nero jumps up and down, pulling me from my memories.

"Yes, of course! You go put your dressing gown on, so you don't get cold, and your trainers, and I'll just check on your sister."

"Quick! Before he goes!"

I pass him his Velcro-fastened trainers and hurry to check on Jasmine. She's fast asleep like an angel. I wonder if it's okay to leave her. I'll only be in the front garden, basically. I don't want to wake her up, it's far too noisy out there. I can keep the baby monitor app open on my phone… I'm sure other parents wouldn't even think twice about it, I'm only overthinking it because she's not mine. It's the added pressure.

"Auntie, hurry up! He's going!"

I hesitate, weighing up the pros and cons. It'll be fine, what's the worst that could happen? I'll only be a few minutes; the windows are locked…

"You be a good girl Jasmine," I whisper, making my decision, and tiptoe back out of the room.

At the bottom of the stairs, Nero stands proudly in his spiderman dressing gown and trainers. His trainers are on the wrong feet but he looks so proud of himself and, as he's in quite a hurry not to miss Father Christmas, I let him go out like that. It's only for a minute. I'm sure his feet won't grow funny in that short of a time. Charlotte will never know.

The door closes softly behind us, unlocked, and I tiptoe in my fluffy socks to the end of the garden path as Nero hurries towards the garishly decorated lorry to join the queue of children in pyjamas.

Looking up at Father Christmas, I can't believe it. It's Jacob Chilbeam, again! Does he never rest? Father Christmas by day and by night? If his charity work is meant to make me hate him less, it doesn't. I still don't like that sandwich-stealer, no matter how famous or great he looks in red.

When it's his turn, Nero goes up the steps of the lorry carefully and I stand proudly with my phone ready to take a photo. I zoom in close so his wrong-footed shoes aren't in the shot, perfect.

Jacob gives me an extra special wave and blows me a kiss. I roll my eyes and usher Nero back towards the house. He's clutching a bag of sweets and is beaming from ear to ear as we retreat down the garden path. My feet are freezing, I should have put shoes on.

"Can I stand and wave until he's gone?" Nero asks.

"You can stand in the warm and wave with the door open. Come on, let's get inside." I push down the door handle and push forwards, but the door doesn't budge. I lift the handle up and push, back down and push, nothing. It's locked. We're locked out. How? I didn't lock it, I let it close. There was no key-turning involved. Jasmine is inside, and we're locked out. Shit. Shit, shit, shit, shit, shit! What if she starts crying? What am I going to do? Did we leave the back door open? Probably not, since it's bloody freezing out here and my toes are about to get frostbite... "Er, Nero, does Mummy leave a spare key outside anywhere? Under a plant pot maybe?"

He looks at me like I've grown two heads.

The lorry has done a loop around the crescent and is now driving past us again, with Nero waving and me franticly willing my sister to answer her bloody phone. She must have a spare key somewhere, right? Maybe one of the neighbours has one? I'm pacing and hopping around almost as much as Nero is because my fluffy socks are now soaking wet ice cubes in the making.

"Auntie, can we go inside now?"

"Yes sweetie, just as soon as I find a key," I smile. His face scrunches up as he considers my words.

"You mean we can't get in?" he asks.

"Well, not right now, but soon. It'll be okay." She must have a friend nearby; someone I can call. If only she would answer her phone and tell me!

34

"But I don't want to stay outside," he whines, panic written all over his face.

"You don't have to, we'll be back inside soon," I try to reassure him.

"I'm coldddd," he whines, pushing his bottom lip out.

"Let's tighten your dressing gown," I say, adjusting his outfit for optimum warmth. What the hell am I going to do?

"Need a hand?" a voice pipes up from behind the bushes.

"Father Kissmas!" exclaims Nero, looking over my shoulder. I can't believe it. I can't flipping believe it. What is up with this guy?

"Well, that depends. Do you have your magic key on you?" I ask, tilting my head and opening my eyes wide with sarcasm.

"No, sadly that's reserved for Christmas Eve use only, but I am rather good at getting in these doors. We had one just like it when I was growing up, you wouldn't believe the number of times I –" he stops himself and I wonder what he was going to say. "Sorry, um, never mind. Let's just say nobody was awake to let me in. Anyway, the point is, I should be able to get this door open for you. Want me to give it a try?"

"Go for it!" I say, guiding Nero out of the way. We stand back and watch as, with a pen in his hand, he manoeuvres most of his arm through the letterbox. It's a larger than standard letterbox, but it's still no mean feat with those biceps. It's all about the angle, it would seem.

"This was a lot easier when I was younger," he admits, twisting around in obvious discomfort. We wait in silence as he twists and groans and oohs and ahhs. Finally, there's a click and the door opens inwards, with Jacob's arm still stuck through the letterbox. Nero rushes inside.

"Are you okay removing yourself or do we need to call the Fire Brigade now?" I tease, holding the door still for him. He manages to free his arm, but it's covered in black marks.

"Thank you for helping us, I was about to have a full-on panic attack! The little one was inside all on her own, how much of a terrible auntie am I?" I start rambling. He touches my hand, sending tingles up my arm.

"Not terrible at all, you're doing a great job."

"Thank you." I don't want to argue because I am doing a great job for somebody who has no experience looking after children. It's only when compared to a regular babysitter that I'm failing abysmally.

I can't stop myself from looking into his kind eyes and at the small section of his face that isn't covered by a fake white beard and Santa hat.

"Wait, shouldn't you be on the lorry?"

He laughs at my concern.

"Nah, that was the end of the route. The lorry is going back without me, the fairy lights and music have been turned off. I said I'd get a taxi back to mine."

"Oh right," I twiddle my fingers. I can't invite him inside my sister's house, can I? Besides, I need to put Nero to bed, and check on Jasmine. Oh my God I still haven't checked on Jasmine! I have allowed myself to get so distracted by this attractive young Father Christmas that I'm neglecting my duties! Still, it's polite to offer. He did do me a massive favour, after all.

"Do you want to come in for a hot chocolate?"

"Do you *want* me to come in?" He's standing so close to me that I wonder whether he's going to lean in for a kiss, but just as he gets within distance, I get a waft.

"Popcorn and cheese," the words slip off my tongue as I think them. Nero was right, this man smells like popcorn and cheese. And just like that, the moment is ruined. I'm back to thinking about that cheese sandwich I didn't get to have, and how selfish this man is. He's probably only doing the Father Christmas stuff to help his image. Charity or otherwise.

"Um, popcorn and what? Sorry I don't get it," he asks.

"It's just something my nephew said. Never mind. I need to put him to bed so er, maybe another time. See ya," I quickly close the door and lock it behind me. *See ya?* What am I, twelve?

*

A few hours later, with both children asleep, I do what any sensible single woman would do. I dig out my unwashed jeans, locate the sexy man's number, and send him a message. Well, I don't want to come across as rude now, do I? That's his trait.

The thing is, it's always hard to stop at just one message. Especially when the other person is this good at flirty banter. I can't help myself, it's natural. It's my instinct kicking in, telling me to get back out there and chase the sexy Santa, to pull down those red crushed velvet, white fur-trimmed trousers and...

"Auntie Abi."

The voice shocks me back into the present and blood rushes to my face as my hand springs back out of my knickers.

"Nero?" I try to regain my composure as I push myself up in bed.

"I miss Mummy. Can I sleep in here peas? Mummy would let me." I raise my eyebrows, but I can't be bothered to argue. He knows I can't check. *Mummy* isn't answering her phone and I'm not sure how much longer I can play her role.

"Sure, come on in," I say, opening the covers for him to join me on the other side of the bed.

"What's that?" he asks, lifting my phone out of his way. On the screen is an image I wish he hadn't seen. It fades to black as the screen finally times out.

"Errrm, it's nothing. Grown up stuff. Come on, let's get comfy and then I'll turn off the light." I say with the straightest face I can manage. My sister is going to kill me.

8

There's something sticky on my cheek, and on my arm, and a little on my thigh. I've had many unfortunate stains on my bedsheets and pyjamas in the past, but nothing quite like this. Although the similarities cannot be denied, these patches have most definitely come from my nephew who is now also known as The Snot Monster.

His face is pink and he's shivering, but to touch he is absolutely boiling. Calpol is the only thing I can think of to do. And to keep Jasmine away from him. If this bug takes out one nibling, it's bad, if it takes out two, it's a disaster.

But what if I catch it?

I've tried calling Charlotte ten times already, and sent messages, but so far, she hasn't replied. I know it's probably only a nasty bug or a cold, kids get sick all the time, but I'd really appreciate some reassurance that I am not about to let my nephew die.

I'm tempted to message Jacob but he's probably the last person who would know what to do, bearing in mind the first time we met, and I don't think we're really at that stage of our relationship. Ha, relationship. A few flirty texts and

I'm already getting carried away. I was the same with Toby and look how that turned out.

Why don't I have any friends with kids that I can ask? I suppose I could Google it, but isn't that what they always say not to do? If I Google it, I'll end up taking him to A&E thinking he's dying when it's really just a cold. I'm sure I should just keep an eye on his temperature, make sure he drinks some water, and rests. Yes. Rest is always a winner. And Calpol, of course. I'll keep him dosed to the recommended amount. That's got to work, right? Rest, water, Calpol, and TV!

We set up a bed on the sofa, bringing Nero's duvet downstairs. I place Jasmine in her own baby-proofed cosy zone of the room, for avoidance of germs, and turn on Disney+ ready to watch one of their favourite Christmas movies for the zillionth time since I got here. Honestly, they won't let me choose, they only want to watch the same movies over and over.

Nero seems very clingy and cuddly despite his high temperature. He's making me burn up too, but at least he seems happier downstairs in front of the TV. I must be doing something right.

*

When my phone vibrates, it wakes me up and I realise both children are asleep. Nero is cuddled into my side, and Jasmine is sleeping in Nero's tiny armchair which is more her size than his. I try to reach for my phone without disturbing anyone, which is easier said than done. I'm millimetres away from it when it vibrates for a second time. *Someone's keen* I joke to myself, sort of hoping it'll be Jacob, but expecting it to be Charlotte.

With my phone finally in my hand, I carefully rest back into position without waking Nero. I've got a message from each of them.

Sorry, can't talk now, I'm on my way to Birmingham. Got a lead on Mike. Sounds like you've got it all in hand, Nero will be fine after a good night's rest or three. Thanks sis x

I roll my eyes at the message. Honestly, one minute she's such an organised 'super mum' type woman with a jam-packed itinerary ready for me, and the next she's so blasé it's frightening.

Next, I open the message from Jacob.

Hey beautiful, just wondered if you and the kids would like to go ice skating? I've got the afternoon off... x

It's a nice offer, but that obviously isn't going to happen today. Besides, I still haven't decided whether to give him a chance, beyond a few cheeky texts. Sure, he saved me by getting us into the house, but that doesn't wash away his initial rude and selfish behaviour. He still stole my sandwich.

I thought you didn't like babies/kids? Anyway, Nero's got a cold so we're not going anywhere. Duvet day. Thanks though, nice idea. X

He replies instantly:

Aw, that's a shame. I hope the little guy feels better soon. Do you need me to drop round any supplies?

I smile. He's so thoughtful, even if he is a bit full on.

I would love some chicken soup, but you'd better not come near us, I don't want you to catch it. You need to stay well until Christmas with all your Father Christmas jobs! Can't have you infecting the entire community!

He replies quickly again.

Yeah, I know. One of the blighters sniffed me the other day!

I snort.

Ah, I think that was Nero. Wanna guess what he said you smelt like?

He doesn't reply straight away, making me wait.

Your next boyfriend? 😌

Oh, he's smooth.

9

A little after 5pm, there's a knock at the door. We're all awake but moving around slowly, exhausted from a day of doing absolutely nothing except rest. Nero is on the sofa, clutching a toy car and watching a different Christmas movie because he was too tired to argue with me, and Jasmine is playing on the carpet. I've just spent 10 minutes staring at the kitchen cupboards for dinner inspiration.

I open the door but there's nobody there, just a couple of tins of chicken soup with red ribbon tied around them in a bow, and an envelope wedged in the middle. I carry them through to the kitchen and then open the envelope. It's a 'Get Well Soon' card for Nero.

I watch the kids playing nicely with each other. Jasmine has pushed herself up to standing and is leaning on the sofa where Nero is lying. He seems to be telling her a story as he pushes his car along the seat cushions, and she watches with adoration. They really are good kids. Char must be doing something right, and I don't seem to have messed them up just yet.

"Hey Nero, Father Christmas' son sent you a 'Get Well Soon' card. Do you want to read it with me?" they both look up at the name 'Father Christmas.' Nero moves his legs a little so I can sit down, and I lift Jasmine up to join us. Nero clasps the card and puts his fingers under the words.

"To Nero," he says confidently. He can't read very well, but he can recognise his name. "I…" his finger hovers under the next word.

"Sound it out," I suggest, with no idea how they teach kids to read these days.

"Her o puh eh," he looks up, frowning.

"Hope."

"You?" he guesses. I nod. "Fer eh eh luh,"

"Feel."

"Buh eh ter ter eh ruh," he looks up.

"Better."

"Can you read the rest?" he begs, his shoulders sagging.

"Okay, but you follow along with me." I hold his hand so I can guide his finger as I read, but I do a quick re-cap to start. "To Nero, I hope you feel better soon. I wondered if you might like to come ice skating with me when you are better. You can bring Auntie Abi and Jasmine, and we can practice ice skating like I do at the North Pole." I pause to allow Nero to gasp. "But not Jasmine, she can play with the other babies as she's too small to go on the ice, not like you. I bet you're going to be a superhero on ice! Make sure your auntie calls me to arrange it the moment you feel better. All the best, Father Christmas (Junior)."

"Can we can we can we?" asks Nero instantly.

"Only once you're better."

"Tomorrow?"

"We'll have to wait and see."

"Peeeeeeas?"

"If I feel your head tomorrow and it's not hot, then maybe. But only if you're well."

"Okay," he says reluctantly, clearly not expecting to make a miraculous recovery.

"Have you heard of magic chicken soup?" I ask him. He shakes his head.

"Well, magic chicken soup can make anyone feel better. Do you want some?"

"Yes peas!"

And with that, my dinner conundrum is solved.

10

"Charlotte, thank goodness you're alive! Where are you?" I balance my phone on the side as I continue to undress Jasmine. I'm getting better at multi-tasking now that I know what I'm doing.

"Of course I'm alive, I'm in Pari'!" she says, putting on a French accent.

"Again? I thought you were going to Birmingham! You do realise it is five days until Christmas, right? As in, you need to be here in three for the Christmas Eve bedtime routine. You promised you'd be back Char, with or without Mike. Nero and Jasmine miss you. When are you coming home? Is it booked at least?"

"I know, I know, don't worry, I'll make it. And I've got loads of souvenirs for Nero and Jasmine, so I'm sure they'll get over it. But listen, I think I've found him. I think he's gone to see the one that got away, you know, his college romance. I was chasing the wrong woman when I came to France the first time, but this is the right one. Her name is Amélie, and I'm certain she has the answers I'm looking for. If I can find her, I'll find him."

"And you're sure that you still want to find him if that's where he is?" I pick up my phone now that Jasmine is fully dressed, and we sit on the floor watching Charlotte flounce around a hotel room.

"Of course I do. I need to talk to him, to remind him how great we are, and to remind him of the kids and, well, mostly to find out why he ran off! We were great. We are great. You know what we're like, we're insufferably perfect. None of this makes any sense unless it's an early mid-life crisis and he's gone to relive his youth with the one that got away, don't you think?"

"And you have this woman's address?"

"His mother had it! See! Proof the whole family is probably disappointed he ended up with me and not the jolie mademoiselle Amélie."

"Er, I'm not sure that's proof Char, but you are coming home straight after you visit her, right? With or without Mike?"

"Yes, yes, don't worry, you won't have to have Christmas without me. I'll be back to tuck Nero in and read 'The Night Before Christmas' and you can finally have a drink!"

"Hey, I've been doing fine on my detox."

"It probably has done you some good. You're like one of those skinny alcoholics."

"Oi! I'm only skinny because I exercise. I still eat!"

"Yeah, yeah, I know. You don't have all the cakes and sweet treats that I do. Hey, how about when I'm back, we do a complete life swap? I can go live at yours and go to the gym or wherever it is you go, and I can go out and have cocktails and flirt with sexy men, and you can carry on playing Auntie Abi."

"No."

"No?" she pulls a face down the camera. "You don't say no to me!"

47

"I do when you're being ridiculous. You love your life, you love these children, and I know that Mike loves you too. He'll reappear with some explanation that you haven't thought of, because I'm certain he's not going to be with Amélie, and you'll go back to being sickeningly perfect before the year is over."

"I see. That's your prediction, huh?"

"It is."

"Well, I hope you're right. But either way, I'm off to see Amélie."

"Be polite!"

"Yes, Dad," she jokes.

"Come say 'bye' to Mummy," I yell to Nero. He rushes over to wave into my phone.

"Bye Mummy, see soon!"

11

"Auntie, it's snowing! Come quick!" Nero exclaims at the foot of my bed before running back out of the room. I push myself up to a seated position and glance at the alarm clock. It's 5am. What was he doing looking out of the window at this hour, watching for snow? He was meant to be resting!

I slide my feet into my slippers and wrap the thick dressing gown I'm borrowing from Charlotte around me as I open the curtains.

He's right. It's still dark out, but there's a clear layer of snow, and more coming from the sky, visible under the glow of the streetlamp.

"Auntie peas hurry up, we need to build a snowman!" Nero returns to my doorway, clasping the cutest pair of Wellington boots I've ever seen.

"I think you need to have your breakfast first; you don't want to get me in trouble, do you?"

"But what if it runs out?" he whines.

Sadly, having experienced many a disappointing British snowfall, I know this to be a possibility even if his terminology is a little off. One minute it looks like snow, the next you have wet mush. Or snow that simply disappears as

49

it lands. It does at least look like we have a small amount to work with if we go outside right now. The snowman will be about ten inches tall, but it will be made of snow. And I'll level up in my Best Auntie rank.

"Okay, I want you to put your boots and your big coat on and your hat and gloves, and I'll get your sister ready in case she wants to play too." I tell him. I also need to find something sensible to wear. At least my bed hair can be hidden under a woolly hat.

"Yay!!!" he skids as he runs back towards his bedroom. I'd better hurry.

I pull on the first pair of jeans and jumper I find, grab my hat and socks, and head into the nursery room where Jasmine is somehow still asleep. Typical. She's only ever asleep when I don't need her to be. I start trying to bundle her into what is best described as a baby space suit without waking her, which works for all of two seconds.

Half an hour later, Jasmine has been fed, changed, and dressed, and Nero is about ready to burst if I don't unlock the back door within the next thirty seconds. As I open it, he flies past me with the speed of a cat or a dog, desperate for freedom. I position Jasmine in her push chair in the corner of the garden, where she can reach out and watch the snow, but not stumble around in it. She seems satisfied with the compromise, which frees me up to assist Nero in his building of a snowman.

I start attempting to roll up a ball of snow across the lawn and instruct Nero to copy me. When I look up, he's lying on the snow moving his arms and legs to make a snow angel. I take a photo and then hold my hand out to help him up.

"We'd better build this snowman quickly, you're going to feel cold now you're all wet," I tell him. He agrees, so we get to work. It isn't until he is positioning some pebbles into our miniature snow man, and I'm standing back to admire our

50

work, that I notice his back. Oh shit. Literally. He must have laid down in snow-covered cat poo when he made the snow angel! It's clear as anything, mushed into his blue coat. I'll have to throw it in the wash. I don't want to be wiping that off by hand.

Is it okay to wash poop-covered clothing in a washing machine?

Back inside, bathed, hair dried and fully warmed up, I consult Charlotte's list for something to do. I don't like driving in snow, no matter how little there is, so it needs to be an 'at home' activity. Otherwise, I'd send Jacob a message about ice skating, because Nero is clearly feeling better. I pick out a couple of options from Charlotte's list.

"Shall we make jam tarts, or paint and decorate paper stockings we can put on the fridge to show Mummy and Daddy?"

"With glitter?" Nero's eyes light up.

"Sure," I say. What's a bit of glitter when you have bogeys under every surface and on bedside walls? It might not be clean, but a bit of sparkle couldn't possibly make this place look any worse…

As it happens, Charlotte has bought glitter pens rather than tubes of loose glitter, so the spread is somewhat controlled. I draw the stocking shapes onto card for each of them to decorate with assorted (washable) paints and glitter pens and a few other sticky back things. Nero can pretty much do his on his own with my supervision, but of course Jasmine requires greater assistance.

Once they've decorated a few each, I leave them to dry before I plan to cut around the outlines later.

"Can we go ice skating now?" asks Nero. I was hoping he'd forgotten about that with the distraction of the snow.

I reach out and touch the back of my palm to his head.

"Hmm, you do feel better," I confirm, "but Auntie doesn't drive in snow, so we can't go today."

"Ohhh," he whines. "Peas? Can Father Kissmas take us?"

"I don't know what kind of car Father Christmas drives," probably some flashy two-seater convertible, "but I can ask, okay?"

"Okay," he agrees politely, then stares at me with expectation. Oh right, he wants me to ask right now. I pick up my phone.

Do I want to ask him? I know we've shared some flirty texts, and he was kind enough to drop off the soup, but if I accept this invitation then it is kind of a date... Am I ready for a date? Like this? A *family* date? Usual dates for me are in coffee shops, cocktail bars, the occasional walk somewhere pretty but popular enough in case it goes badly. Usual dates are not romantic ice skating in the snow situations, with or without children in tow.

Will he hold my hand whilst we skate? Will he help me up if/when I fall? Will he brush off my icy wet bum?

"Well?" Nero prompts. Jeez, he gets his impatience from his mother. I finally send a text explaining that Nero is better and would love to go ice skating but that I don't like driving in the snow, so maybe he could pick us up.

"I'll tell you when he replies. Go play with your cars."

12

Okay, so I was wrong about the flashy convertible. It turns out, Jacob drives a perfectly normal Volkswagen Passat and we arrived at the temporary ice rink like a regular family of four. It was quite a bizarre feeling. I would have worn a sign on my head to tell people it's not what it looks like except, deep down (like, really deep down) I actually, kind of, liked it. Just don't tell Charlotte, okay? This isn't my lifestyle at all, I don't *do* family stuff. I do friends stuff and date stuff, not family hand/mitten holding on ice stuff. And for a guy who supposedly doesn't like babies, Jacob seems to be enjoying himself too.

We've passed Jasmine over to his friend Josie who has a little creche running at the side of the rink, and the three of us are on the ice, holding hands and wobbling over like every other family out here. It's fun! Nero has a lot more confidence than I do, wanting to prove Father Christmas right by being a "superhero on ice." He keeps trying to speed up, but I'm afraid to let go of his hand in case he falls and has his fingers chopped off by a passing skater.

As it's getting later, the music has turned to Bublé rather than cheesy Christmas music, and with the twinkly lights surrounding the rink and a very poor attempt at snow coming from the sky, it feels romantic. Jacob is confident and smooth on the ice. He's clearly had practice, unlike me.

Finally, Nero is worn out and ready to stop. We skate to the side. Before I can follow him off the rink, Jacob calls out to Josie to see if she can keep an eye on Nero too, just for a minute. I don't even hear her response before he twirls me around, his hands on the barrier either side of me.

"One more round, just us?" he asks, with that undeniable twinkle in his eye.

He takes my hand once more and leads me further onto the ice. He guides me at a faster speed but in such a smooth and caring way. His arm moves to my side, resting gently on my hip, making us move as one. I no longer feel afraid. I feel safe beside him. I feel warm, cared for, and-

Oh dear, there's a child on the floor. Repeat: there is a child on the floor. We need to divide to go around him. I let go of Jacob and flounder my way around the boy, narrowly avoiding his fingers. My legs are out of control, I desperately try to right my balance as my body threatens to fall forwards then backwards. I aim for the side of the rink but before I reach it, a familiar arm draws me back towards him and my body is thrown into his. By some miracle, we don't topple over and instead find ourselves stopped still, coat to coat. The closest we have ever been.

It seems weird seeing him without his fake white beard; seeing his face like it was on the TV, only better. His eyes seem to show genuine care that I never anticipated, his smile causes real dimples in his cheeks, and his aftershave... oh who am I kidding? The boy was right, this man smells like popcorn and cheese, and I just want a taste!

"Auntie!!!!" I hear the familiar cry. The moment is over.

"Jacob, you told me she was potty-trained! This little lady has been stinking out all of the other children, and I have nobody here who can change her! Please take her out of here immediately!" Josie bellows, her face red with anger.

"I'm so sorry! It won't happen again!" shouts Jacob with a grin. I grab Jasmine as soon as I have kicked off my ice skates, stepping in icy puddles in my socks. It didn't feel appropriate to enter the creche wearing blades on my feet.

"I'm sorry, he didn't tell me she wasn't allowed," I tell Josie as I pass by, trying not to linger any longer than absolutely necessary, because Jasmine really does stink. "Thank you for keeping an eye on her."

"Ah, don't worry about it. He's a charmer that one, I'm always doing him favours, but he keeps his word, you know? I saw you both out on the ice, looking rather cosy together. Is there something cooking between you?" she asks as she gathers some tiny discarded socks from the floor.

"Oh, I dunno," I shrug. "It's early days."

"Well, if you want my input, I'd say give him a chance. If the guy's putting up with that stench," she eyes Jasmine, "he must like you, a lot." I laugh awkwardly and slip out of the exit.

Once Jasmine has been changed and the stench is gone, Jacob drops us back home. He can't come in because he's got more Father Christmas duties to carry out tonight, but I thank him for taking us out and silently wonder if I'll ever see him again.

If Charlotte were to come back tonight, and I went back to the city, would that be it? Over before it started, before I even got to taste those lips?

13

The next evening, at the end of another action-packed day, we have a right treat on our itinerary: Carols by Candlelight at the local church. The priest will be leading a nativity service suitable for children followed by lots of carol singing. It's not my idea of fun. The kids aren't that fussed about going either (because Jasmine has no opinion and goes wherever I push or carry her) and Nero doesn't want to go anywhere that he can't bring a toy car. I'm not entirely sure if toy cars are permitted in church, but I decided not to let him bring one as I didn't want him pushing it and losing it under a pew or the altar or something. I could do without damning myself by crossing holy thresholds or breaking unspoken rules, or whatever… I haven't been to church since I left secondary school, around the time I met my first serious boyfriend and waved goodbye to my virginity.

We approach the somewhat grey church on foot, and I can't help but feel that a few fairy lights here and there would have been a good idea to help the place seem more inviting to the children so clearly targeted for this service. Instead, it feels more like we're walking towards a candlelit séance on hallowed ground. I tighten my grip on Nero.

As we walk through the arched entrance, an organ springs into life, playing a slow rendition of 'Away in a Manger.' Instead of listening to my subconscious, which screams "RUN!!!", we follow the designated path and soon find a special area of the church where it is clearly intended for the younger children to sit. A couple of mums are already sat there with their children, any partners presumably on the pews with the rest of the congregation. I park the pushchair at the side, as out of the way as I can, and unclip Jasmine so that we can all sit down together. Turns out, the carpet does nothing to soften the stone floor underneath, and it's rather cold. Isn't this how you get piles?

Nero nudges me because some of the other children have toys, so he could have brought his car, but I refuse to argue and instead distract him with a game of I-Spy.

"I spy with my little eye, something beginning with…" I search around for something easy for him to guess, "b."

"Boy?"

"No."

"Baby?"

"No." (But why didn't I think of that?)

"Bbbbbumble bee?" I tilt my head at him and raise my eyebrows,

"No."

"It's too hard!" he scrunches up his little fists indignantly.

"Keep guessing," I tell him and he takes a good hard look around the church.

"Book!" he exclaims confidently. I was going for Bible, but I'll accept book as I don't know what he's been taught yet.

"Well done! Your turn." He doesn't seem to need to think at all.

"I got a good one Auntie."

"Okay, you say the words then."

"I spy with my little eyes, something beginning with 'c' no 'f' ffff."

I instantly realise he's spotted Father Christmas, but that doesn't make any sense. We're in a church, this is not Father Christmas territory! This is a Christian service supposed to educate children about the nativity, so I highly doubt they've thrown in a Father Christmas to confuse matters. There's no North Pole in the nativity; it's all about Bethlehem, a much warmer destination.

I look around to see if somebody has brought a toy Father Christmas with them, or maybe someone's wearing a Christmas jumper with him on, and then I clock him. Father Christmas a.k.a. Jacob Chilbeam, the text flirter and ice skater extraordinaire himself. He's not dressed in red tonight, he's wearing a navy high-neck jumper with a short zip at the top, as far as I can tell from here. He raises his arm and waves at me as I pull my eyes away.

I turn back to Nero,

"Father Christmas," I guess.

"Wow!!! You're so good. That was a hard one," Nero tells me. Hmm, a hard one indeed, my mind retorts inappropriately. NO. I stop myself. I am in church for crying out loud, I can't be having dirty thoughts like that in here. Lord only knows what might happen to me. I'm here to teach these children about Jesus' birth, no matter my personal beliefs. I shift on the floor uncomfortably.

Does his presence mean that Jacob is a Christian? A practising Christian? I can't decide if I want him to be one or not. On one hand, I like to believe all Christians are good, kind-hearted people. On the other, some of the bitchiest girls in my school were practising Christians, and their parents were even worse. Less 'God loves everyone equally' and more 'he loves us more, that's why we're rich and live in a big house, and you must not be worthy or good enough and that's why your mum left you and you live in a flat.' They constantly reminded me that my home was smaller than theirs and that I didn't have a mum. As if I could forget.

It was just me, Charlotte, and Dad for almost as long as I can remember. Mum ran off to be happy with some other guy, to have a new family. Dad tried his best to raise us whilst I picked up the slack as Big Sister, and then he died of lung cancer about five years ago. He'd ignored the signs until it was too late. But this isn't a sob story, I don't want to talk about that. My life is totally fine, I'm okay, when I'm not being dumped and having my heart broken or freezing my butt off sitting on thinly covered concrete in church.

But Jacob, now there's a puzzle. A flirty texter, great at banter, kind eyes, and seemingly good intentions, playing Father Christmas now but was on 'Love Under The Stars' and he smells like popcorn and cheese. He seems a little too good to be true. I don't normally go for nice guys, never mind ones who start off as arrogant sandwich-stealers and then become nice over time. I don't know what to make of him, I'm not sure which side of him is real. The TV star, the sandwich-stealer, or the kind-hearted man who doesn't mind hanging out with me and my niblings?

As the service begins, I feel a vibration in my bum bag. Oh yes, I'm wearing a bum bag, I came prepared. I have all sorts of essentials resting on my stomach today. But I can't check my phone when I'm sat only a couple of metres away from a very serious-looking priest. Nero is picking at the carpet, and his nose, and Jasmine is sucking her hand. I don't want to draw any more attention to our behaviour, or we might be kicked out.

It vibrates again. I focus on the priest's words, trying not to wonder if it's Jacob texting me. He's not a very good Christian at all if he's picked up where we left off last night, in the house of God of all places. I try to sneak a look at him and catch his eye. He smiles. Oh, I am in danger with this one.

I can already see myself dating him and falling for him all before having my heart broken again in approximately five months' time. You think I'm cynical, but it's happened so many times now, it's no longer a joke. But how can I stop repeating the cycle? I need to keep trying, right? How will I know when I've found the guy who isn't going to leave me or hurt me, if I don't give them all a chance? It's a blinking catch-22 situation unless I want to end up alone forever.

Buzz.

It's got to be him. He knows I can't look, and he's vibrating my bum bag for fun. That naughty man. I look over at him again, and he's still looking at me.

"Auntie?" Nero says.

"Shh! We can't talk whilst the priest is talking," I whisper, holding a finger to my mouth.

"But…" he whines as I shake my head at him and then he rolls his eyes. He looks so much like his mum right now.

When the priest finishes talking and hands over to somebody else to lead the carol singing part of this gathering, Nero taps my arm.

"Can I talk now?"

People have already started singing and we're meant to be singing too.

"Not really, but tell me quickly."

He kneels up and prepares to shout into my ear,

"Can Father Kissmas come to our house tonight?" he pulls away, grinning.

"It's not Christmas Eve," I tell him. He kneels back up,

"Not *real* Father Kissmas, his son, the one that likes you."

I narrow my eyes at him, the four-year-old matchmaker.

"Why do you want him to come round?"

"Because he *likes* you and you need a boyfriend, Auntie Abi."

"Who says I need a boyfriend?" I ask, not worried that we're talking over the singing anymore.

"Mummy." Of course.

"What exactly did Mummy say?"

"Mummy said you need help picking a good boyfriend. So, I picked. He's a good one, I know!" he beams, clearly very proud of himself.

"How do you know he's a good one?"

"Because he's Father Kissmas! And he smells like popcorn and cheese. No baddies smell like popcorn and cheese."

"Oh really? What do baddies smell like then?" I ask.

"They smell like… onions!" he giggles. "So, can he come round? Peas!"

"Well, I don't know. What do you think, Jasmine?" I bend to the side to get a look at her face. She reaches her arms up, bends her knees and starts sort of boogeying on the floor. I take that as a 'yes', she's fully on board with her brother's plan (and is simultaneously enjoying 'Hark! The Herald Angels Sing').

I unzip my bum bag, reach in, and unlock my phone. Sure enough, three messages from Jacob.

Didn't expect to see you here.

Wanna do something after?

Maybe we could talk once the kids are in bed?

Well, he's certainly keen. It's a bit of a red flag for me though, like, why is he so interested in me? I'm a nobody babysitting her sister's young kids, I can't possibly be the

62

most appealing option in town. But, at least I can blame Nero if it all goes wrong. And then myself, for following the advice of a four-year-old. A very wise four-year-old, who smells people.

Popcorn and cheese, honestly. I really need to ask Jacob about that. Like, does he bathe in the stuff? And, I know what you're thinking: cheese can't be a good thing to smell of. You're thinking of cheesy feet. But throw in some popcorn scent too, and it's a cosy inviting smell. Comforting, like mac 'n' cheese, with popcorn. Cinema, but at home. I don't know, it's weird, but it's my kind of weird. I like it.

I reply:

As it happens, Nero just invited you round. How do you fancy finally having that hot chocolate I offered you?

He replies almost instantly.

I'll meet you in the graveyard when this finishes. Not in a creepy way, there's just no other exit.

I laugh.

I know, churches are creepy AF! But maybe that's 'cause I'm a sinner. Are you a good Christian boy?

I can't resist a cheeky flirt.

You'll have to wait to find out.

He sends it with a devil emoji. I put my phone away and tell Nero the good news. Not that he'll get to see him for long though, it's nearly bedtime. And then it will be just us adults. The horny teenager in me squeals.

Me and Jacob Chilbeam from *'Love Under The Stars'*! Oh, if that blushing teenager from the grotto could see me now!

I feel like we should pull out a blow-up mattress and a double sleeping bag and toast marshmallows in the garden. I can't believe this is my life!

14

"Okay, that's it. They're in bed," I say to the gorgeous man currently occupying my sister's sofa as I close the door behind me. It feels naughty having him here, like I've invited a boy to come over whilst my parents are out. Dad never had a clue what I got up to when he was putting in extra hours at work. I was in charge of Charlotte, and I paid for her silence with M&M's.

"I hope you don't mind, I went ahead and made the hot chocolate," he says, indicating two mugs topped with squirty cream. Beside them lies a bowl of popcorn.

"And popcorn?"

"Yeah, sorry. I'm a bit of an addict. At least it's not drugs, right?" he pulls a face and I laugh.

"Absolutely," I reach for a handful. It's salted, so we have a perfect balance of sweet hot chocolate and savoury salted popcorn. Mmm. I move further back on the sofa beside him with my feet up and then turn to face him better.

"So, I'm just going to come right out and ask... why me? Why are you even entertaining the possibility of dating me, when you're a hot reality star who must have way better options than some woman who's looking after her sister's kids?"

"Have you looked in the mirror lately?"

I laugh nervously in response. Yes, I have, and I recall that on the day we met, I had matted hair caused by an unknown substance. I don't anymore, but that's beside the point. We all know first impressions are everything.

"You're hot, Abi. But this isn't even about looks. Honestly, I know a bit about you. I knew your dad."

"Really? How?" I frown. It's hard enough to believe he finds me attractive, but him knowing my dad is just plain weird.

"My dad worked with him, and I interned at the office during a couple of summers. He was a great guy, and he was so proud of you, you know. The way you still stuck at it and achieved everything you wanted to, mum or no mum."

Wow.

His words hit me right in the throat, I wasn't expecting that. I struggle to swallow my mouthful of popcorn. I thought he was going to say he met my dad at the supermarket, or in the queue at the bank, and perhaps he'd whipped out a photo of me from his wallet. My dad was known for being quite chatty with strangers sometimes, but he didn't usually talk about real things. He didn't talk about us, not our achievements nor our aspirations. Nothing beyond our ages and existence. I'm not even sure he knew which A-Levels I took.

My dad was great at small talk, the weather, local news. He never told me he was proud of me, so I can't believe that he told some random man's son at work. I don't know what to say. The popcorn refuses to leave my mouth. Fortunately, Jacob continues.

"When I heard about his diagnosis and later his passing, I wanted to reach out and contact you. I know it sounds weird, but I'd sat at his desk sometimes, I'd seen photos of you and your sister. I felt like I knew you." He clears his throat. "Of course, that was a while ago now, and I didn't act on it. And I didn't recognise you at the shopping centre, I swear. I was blinded by hanger, my stomach rumbling out of control. It wasn't until later, when I looked you up – after I gave you my number – that I realised I knew exactly who you were. And it seemed kind of like fate had brought us together. Do you believe in fate?"

"I don't know what to say." I sip my hot chocolate, finally ridding my mouth of popcorn.

"Sorry," he says sheepishly. "So, what do you want to know about me? It seems only fair, since I had a head start learning about you."

"Well, I had a head start too. I watched you on '*Love Under The Stars*'." I smile and he runs his fingers through his hair and sighs.

"Worst decision of my life. If you ever want to make someone feel like complete and utter shite, sign them up for a reality dating show, and the trolls will do the rest. I had death threats. I had messages accusing me of taking steroids. People judging me for the slightest opinions I expressed on the show, blowing them way out of proportion. And the producers didn't care, they made it worse. They just want ratings. There's a list of therapists provided to everyone at the start because they know we're going to need them, and that's it. The price of fame. And I wasn't even doing it for the fame!"

"What were you doing it for then? Love?"

"No, I'm not that gullible. I was doing it for the money. I support a homeless charity and I thought it was a good idea, because of the tents… I know, it's a tedious link, but I thought it would be great exposure for the charity if I won. Sadly, none of the girls were interested in teaming up with me for charity, they wanted the money for themselves. That's why nobody picked me in the end; they knew I wasn't serious about finding love or pretending to for national TV, and once they got wind that I planned to give the winning money to charity instead of splitting it and spending it on unnecessary extravagances or furthering our careers, they all gave me a wide berth."

"I had no idea."

"Yeah, that didn't make the show. But that's why I'm here now, playing Father Christmas. I'm trying to raise funds for that same homeless charity again. It means a lot to me."

"Can I ask why that charity in particular?" I move closer to him as I place my mug back down on the table.

"It was… I was…" Jacob stumbles over his words, so I look up and am surprised to find his eyes are watery, cheeks flushed. "My dad and I, before he met your dad, we… we lived in a shelter. My dad was a mess, a recovering alcoholic, we got kicked out of our rented flat and we had nowhere else to go. But your dad took us under his wing, he ensured my dad got a job in his office – even lent him a suit to wear for the interview – and that was all we needed. A chance. Somebody to believe in us. My dad was already incentivised to change, he just didn't know how. It seems impossible, you know, when you have nothing. It's much easier to give up than to keep trying. Your dad was the only one who believed in him, and he's the only reason we're both still around today. I truly believe that. My dad was probably months, weeks, even days away from suicide when they met, and what would have happened to me? The care system if I was lucky. If not, a child living on the streets alone. I wouldn't have made it."

My skin has goosebumps; I'm shaken, heartbroken for him. I knew my dad was a kind man, but I had no idea how much he'd helped others. He was always so overwhelmed at home, he relied on me to help with Charlotte. I am stunned to learn that he helped this father and son whom he didn't even know. Of course, now that I know, it sounds so much like him. But why didn't he say anything? Why didn't he tell us what he'd done?

"You didn't know?" Jacob asks, more of a statement than a question.

"I had no idea, he never said anything. Did you or your dad come to the funeral?"

Jacob shakes his head.

"My dad sent flowers, but he wasn't able to make the service."

"I can't believe it. I mean, I can, but wow." This is not how I thought tonight would go. Both of us look far too teary for a date.

"Here, finish your hot chocolate before it goes cold," Jacob passes my mug and I hold it with both hands and stare into it. I feel like my heart just got broken and mended again in the space of two minutes. My dad. My good, honest, kind dad. He saved their lives, but he didn't brag, he didn't even mention it. He was deserted by his wife, but he still helped those struggling even more than himself. Dad. Oh, Dad. The tears finally spill down my cheeks.

Jacob moves my mug back out of the way and pulls me into his arms. I take a deep inhale of his scent. Without my

69

dad, this man might not be alive right now. He definitely wouldn't be the man he is today. This is not at all the love story I was expecting to write with this reality star, this is deep. I cry into his shoulder.

Finally, when my breathing steadies again, I lean back, keeping my arms around him. He wipes beneath my eyes with his thumb, and I look at him, really look at him. This man is so much more than that nice bum I saw on the telly, this man is real. Three dimensional. This man just let me in. He just told me something more personal than the last six men I dated. And my dad…

Before I can start crying again, Jacob moves closer. I can barely breathe, my eyes wide with attraction. I close them as his lips connect with mine, sending fireworks to my heart. This is what it's meant to feel like. This is two people connecting. Fuuuudge, I want him so badly!

We fondle and kiss and caress all over my sister's sofa like two horny teenagers, but we don't go all the way. It's too soon, and it feels wrong with the kids upstairs. I want to do this right. Jacob senses my resistance.

"I should be going," he says, pulling away.

"I want to do this properly. I want to get to know you. To know if this is real…" I tell him and he kisses me again.

"Me too."

He stands, straightens his clothes and moves towards the door.

"Wait!" I say, surprising myself. "When can I see you again?"

"Well, I'm busy right up until Christmas, but I'm sure we can figure something out. You've got my number. I'm not letting you get away that easily!" he winks and then grins. I stand up and pull him into a hug.

"Good! Because I think I might like you."

"I think I might like you too," he teases back before kissing me on the forehead and letting himself out.

I slide down the closed door and sit on the floor with a smile on my face like a girl in one of those cheesy movies. What have I got myself into?

15

"Oh my God, Charlotte! Finally! I have so much to tell you!" I babble into the phone the second she answers it. I can't wait to tell her all about Jacob. "But actually, before I say anything, please tell me you're on your way home?"

"Why, what is it? Are the kids okay?"

"They're fine, Nero's great, back to normal. In fact, it turns out he's a bit of a matchmaker…" I pull a face at my phone.

"What do you mean? I hope you haven't been going on dates with my children, Abi. That's not okay."

"I'm not saying another word until you tell me you're on your way home." I threaten.

"Spill it sis, you wouldn't have called me if you didn't want to tell me. I am on my way home; I'm just having some slight delays…"

"Charlotte, no! You promised! You have to get back in time!"

"Don't you think I'm trying?" she retorts angrily. "Now spill the goss or I'm hanging up."

I sigh, what a drama queen. She's totally spoilt the moment.

"Nero picked a date for me." I pause for dramatic effect. "Father Christmas, or 'Father Kissmas' as he calls him."

"Huh?"

"Your sexy Santa from the shopping centre, Jacob Chilbeam from '*Love Under The Stars.*' Turns out he has a bit of a thing for me." I tell her, stealing myself for an amazing reaction.

"Whatttttt????"

"But it gets better than that, okay. You are not going to believe this."

"It gets better than dating or even flirting with a hot z-list celebrity?" she asks, incredulous. "Did he introduce you to Zac Efron? Ryan Reynolds? Chris Hemsworth?" I roll my eyes at her ridiculous ideas.

"He knew Dad."

"Huh? I don't get it. Why's that such a good thing? Bit weird, isn't it?"

"No. Last night we had such an amazing heart-to-heart and as much as I learnt about Jacob and his background, I learnt about Dad too. Did you know that he helped a homeless man with a son get a job so they could get themselves out of a shelter? That son was Jacob. And when he grew up, he interned at the office, and got to know Dad! There was this whole other side to Dad that we never knew about. I can't believe it, it all feels a bit like…"

"Fate?" she interrupts.

"Yeah." I smile. "Do you think I'm being crazy?"

"I think you're following your heart again, like you always do. You always chase love and I just hope that this time it works out for you. He is a z-list celebrity, he must have all sorts of opportunities open to him at the moment. Be careful."

"But that's just it! He isn't arrogant like I thought he was at first, he was just hangry! He's doing all this Father

Christmas stuff for charity, he even went on '*Love Under The Stars*' for charity - because he wants to raise money for the homeless shelter he stayed in as a child. He's a good guy, Char. I think I might have finally found a good guy."

"Well, I hope one of us has," she says, turning the conversation back to her. It's standard Charlotte behaviour, I know she's only jealous.

"Why, what's happened now?"

"I still haven't found Mike. He wasn't with Amélie, who by the way was every bit the b-i-t-c-h I was expecting, none of his friends are responding to me, his parents haven't heard anything, and I've been everywhere I can think of. I'm out of leads. I don't know where else to look."

"But you are coming home now, right? You can't waste any more time searching, your kids need you. And besides, I'm sure Mike will come back eventually."

"I won't sit at home and wait like Dad did. Mum never came home, did she? So, what if Mike doesn't? What if this is it? I've had my years of wedded bliss, and now it's my turn to be a single mum of two. I can't do single life, Abi, I'm not strong like you."

"Oh yeah, because I'm such an expert," I retort.

"You are so good at brushing yourself off and starting again. I don't know how you do it. I don't have that strength."

"Yes, you do. If you needed to do it, you would find the strength. But I really don't think you're going to need to. Mike is going to come back, I know it."

"But how can you be so sure?"

"Because I've seen the way he looks at you and the kids. No man has ever looked at me that way… until last night."

"Oh jeez, Abi, you've got it bad. Just don't forget to look after my kids whilst you're daydreaming about your new lover, okay? I'll see you soon."

"Wait-" I start, but she's already ended the call. When exactly is she coming home? It's Christmas Eve tomorrow!

I put my phone down on the carpet and turn Jasmine to face me.

"What are we gonna do, Jazzy-Ju?"

"Auntie, come quick! Elfward had an accident again!" Nero beckons me from the doorway. What now?

16

I take back everything I previously thought about Charlotte's house being a bit of a mess when I arrived, it was practically spotless compared to how it is now. As the days have progressed, my initial habit of tidying up toys at the end of each day has gone completely awry.

And now Nero, aided by the mischievous Elfward, has had another accident. I suppose it's my own fault for putting the idea into his head that the elf could bake. It's all been downhill since then, 'accidents' everywhere.

There is a jam tart stuck to a sofa cushion, orange cheese puff powder ground into the grey carpet, Lego and toy cars literally everywhere you look - including half-way up the Christmas tree and parked at the back of the toilet – and Nero seems to have chocolate smeared around his mouth all day every day excluding about 30 minutes after his teeth are brushed in the morning and evening. I don't even know where the chocolate is coming from at this point, just that I haven't found it all.

That started as a fun 'treasure hunt' and then Nero offered to hide more chocolate than I initially did, so that we could play every day. I thought he was just going to take a few more chocolates off the tree, but it seems he must have found a hidden stash I wasn't aware of, because there are chocolate buttons everywhere, in various states of stickiness, along with those foil-wrapped chocolate coins and the odd jelly sweet. None of which could I find when I went hunting for goodies soon after I arrived, when I suffered my first sugary cocktail cravings, hence my suspicion that a secret stash has been uncovered. If I find M&M's next, I'll know it's Charlotte's and then I'm in big trouble. I'd better clean up this mess and re-stock the secret stash before she gets back.

Nero walks up to me with his hands on his hips like a mini-Charlotte. He sighs.

"Auntie, we need to tidy up," he says, completely seriously, like a little old man.

"Will you help me?" I ask him. He nods. "I keep Smean out of the way."

It's not the kind of help I was after, but I'll take it. I stand up and try to motivate myself to get stuck in. If a four-year-old is saying we need to tidy up, it must be bad. I put on a Christmas playlist and start by clearing the floor of toys.

It is hours before I can finally sit back down and check my phone. Both children are asleep, and the elf is in a custom-made jail cell for the night. I exchange a few cheeky texts with Jacob, and then I get myself ready for bed, dreading tomorrow. I thought they'd both be back by now.

17

Christmas Eve

Christmas Eve. It's Christmas Eve. I am not prepared for this. I can't read 'The Night Before Christmas' and sneak around placing presents under the tree tonight. I can't take a bite out of a mince pie or a cookie, or have a swig of some milk, and then wake up in the morning and act like everything is magical and like there aren't two very important people missing. Nero is going to bawl his eyes out worse than Jasmine if they don't get back today. Charlotte assured me that she would be back in time for Christmas, with or without Mike, but her last call wasn't particularly reassuring.

Nero's excitement for Christmas is off the charts thanks to the children's TV programmes all upping the ante, and the only thing we have to do today, besides the general 'Christmas fun' that we have been having every day since I got here (such as craft time, movie time, and gingerbread decorating), is to purchase a carrot for Rudolph.

Now, I'm no fool, I've seen the adverts, I know you can get carrot sticks from McDonalds these days, so there's no need to go shopping on Christmas Eve. But Nero has assured me that those are not good carrots, because they are too small. He doesn't want prepared carrot batons, he wants one of those ugly fresh out of the ground carrots, all bumpy and in need of peeling, and he wants to choose it himself. I just hope I don't need to give evidence of consumption, like bite marks, on that gross carrot because otherwise I'm going to need to get creative with a knife. I certainly have no desire to bite it like that. Hairy, raw carrots are not my snack of choice!

So anyway, that is why, after Nero's morning poop and wipe – an event for all, I can assure you – we have wrapped ourselves up in our winter coats with hats and scarves, Jasmine has been bundled into her pushchair, and we are now making our way towards the local shops hoping that the greengrocers is open. I thought walking would help to burn some of their excited energy.

We can see our answer from down the street: the greengrocers is heaving, with queues out onto the pavement. Customers are buying their vegetables for tomorrow's roast dinner, and it occurs to me that I should probably buy some extra veg too because if by some miracle Charlotte does turn up in time for the morning present-opening, she is unlikely to come via a shop. Plus, I should be prepared to cook a roast dinner, just in case.

With Nero's help, I bag up some broccoli, Brussels sprouts, and plenty of carrots, keeping the one for Rudolph separate to avoid any confusion or accidental cooking. It's not like I'm going to be cooking them until after Rudolph's supposed visit, so Nero could just pick one out of the bag when we get back, but I suppose we don't want him forgetting which one he chose. Heaven forbid we should eat Rudolph's carrot instead of our own! I suppose I've got to keep humouring him, so he doesn't get upset that his parents appear to have abandoned him at the most special time of the year.

I do love my sister, but she really hasn't handled this situation well at all. I'd never say it to her face, but her leaving Nero here with me reeks of what Mum did to us. I can't believe she's done it. She knows what it feels like to have your excitement tinged with fear; to feel happy that it's nearly Christmas, excited that you might see your mum, and sad that you might never see her again. I know I'm here to ensure Nero doesn't get upset about it, but there's no denying the facts, and he's a smart little man.

When we get back to the house, Nero helps me decorate a gingerbread house. Or rather, he decorates the pieces (coats with icing and sweets) and then I attempt to stick them all together in the shape of a house. I can honestly say I've never built a gingerbread house before, but I think we manage a pretty decent job. It's slightly wonky, but there's a lot of icing and sweets stuck on, so I'm confident that it will taste good. I'm not sure what the process is when it comes to eating it though… do we smash it, or what?

We settle down in front of the TV and my phone buzzes. I grab it to see if it's Charlotte finally telling me she's on her way home. Nope, Jacob again. I place my phone back on the side without replying. I don't want to be too keen; my feelings are already overwhelming me, and I barely even know the man.

The hours pass with relative ease and laziness, and at bedtime, there's still no sign of Charlotte or Mike. We set out the treats for Father Christmas and Rudolph, and then I lead a very excited Nero up to bed.

"Do you think I'll hear his sleigh on the roof?" he asks, looking at his ceiling.

"No, because you'll be asleep. Remember, he only comes if you're asleep," I warn him.

"But what if I pretend?"

"He'll know, and then you'll end up on the naughty list. You don't want that, do you?"

"No!" he shakes his head repeatedly.

"Good, so snuggle down then and listen to this story and then go to sleep like a good boy."

"Okay, Auntie."

I read 'The Night Before Christmas' and then, before I can leave the room, Nero asks to make a Christmas wish. It seems to be an idea he's picked up somewhere, rather than one Charlotte has encouraged. There wasn't any mention of a Christmas wish on her list. He puts his hands together as if in prayer.

"I wish for Mummy and Daddy to come home, for scaticks, and something for Smean. And I wish for Auntie Abi to be boyfriend and girlfriend with Father Kissmas' son," he opens his eyes and I tickle him under his armpits.

"Alright you cheeky matchmaker!" I let him calm down again and then re-tuck the covers how he likes. "Night, night. Sleep tight. Tomorrow, it's Christmas!"

"Yay!" he squeals. "And Mummy and Daddy will be home!"

"That's right," I smile and pull the door almost closed behind me. He doesn't like it fully closed.

18

I've learnt a lot about that little man in there, dreaming about seeing his mummy and daddy and getting Scalextric for Christmas. He's such a cool little dude. I hope Charlotte and Mike aren't about to mess him up for good by not showing up in time.

I use a step so I can reach the top of Charlotte's built-in wardrobe, where she has hidden most of their presents in black sacks. Fortunately, they're already wrapped and just need placing under the tree, with a few smaller ones stuck into a stocking we have laid out by the electric fireplace. I hold as much as I can carry and take them downstairs before returning for the rest. There's rather a lot! I wonder if they're overcompensating for something... are they not as happy as I was led to believe?

Once I've positioned the presents, I sit back and admire my hard work. Not only is the house relatively tidy, but it looks incredibly festive with all of our homemade decorations scattered about, and the presents look sufficiently overwhelming for Nero to get excited about in the morning. I curl up under a throw blanket and reach for the plate of cookies. This is definitely one perk of being the only adult in the house on Christmas Eve!

I eat the cookies, careful to leave plenty of crumbs on the plate, whilst I scroll through my recent messages. I still haven't replied to Jacob. I know that I need to, that I shouldn't leave him hanging when things were going so well, but if I'm being honest and not putting on my usual "I'm fine" face – I'm scared. I don't know if I'm ready to open myself up to getting hurt again. I really like him, and I think I've finally forgiven him for the whole sandwich-stealing incident (we've all been hangry, I get it) but I'm scared. I don't want to get hurt again. Maybe it's safer to just stay single, you know? Charlotte thinks I'm so good at brushing myself off and starting again, but it does take a toll on me each time. I don't know how many more times I can do it before I swear off men entirely.

I take a swig of milk, leaving a little at the bottom of the glass, and then I take the carrot to the kitchen. I am not taking a bite out of that hairy monstrosity. I get to work with a shaped pastry cutter before disposing of the evidence.

With that, my job is complete, so I put myself to bed and try to get an early night. I can't believe Charlotte isn't back yet. I send her one final text for good measure. She'd better be here by morning.

*

At 10:15pm, there's a key in the lock. Oh my God, there's a key in the lock! Somebody's home! I tiptoe down the first few stairs and then nearly fall down the rest as the light is suddenly turned on and Mike walks right into me.

"Whoa – What are you doing here? You made me jump!" he exclaims. I hold my finger to my mouth and indicate that we should move to the lounge; we don't want to wake Nero.

Sitting on the sofa, I curl my feet up and nurse my Lego-inflicted wounds. That's something I won't miss when I return to normal life, treading on Lego in the dark.

"First things first, where have you been?" I demand as if he's a teenager attempting to sneak in after curfew. He frowns at me.

"What do you mean, where have I been? I went to Prague on a stag do, then over to Germany to pick this up for Nero," he unzips his luggage and pulls out some kind of fancy toy car. I'm sure Nero's going to love it, even if I don't appreciate its greatness. "I told Charlotte what I was doing."

"Well, she thinks you ran off. She's been searching everywhere for you, even France, and she still isn't back."

"What do you mean, she thinks I ran off? I told her where I was going!"

"Did you though? How many times? Was she listening?"

"I told her when she was cooking dinner one night. I explained the plan, I said it tied in really well with flights and that I'd be back, well, *now*. Just in time to wrap this up ready for the morning. But if she thinks I left her…" he clasps his head and looks down as if stretching his neck, then looks up at me and frowns, "why would she think that? We're great together."

"Well, maybe if you had called or text…" I suggest.

"Ah yeah, well, I left my phone in my car at the airport because I was in such a hurry, and I don't know her number off by heart. But I did send an email. Didn't she check her emails?"

"Which email address did you use?"

"Her usual one, you know, whiskersonkittens." I shake my head at him with pity.

"I don't think she's used that account since she finished Uni."

"Oh. But still, just because I didn't message, doesn't mean she should immediately assume that I've run away. We have a good solid marriage. What is she playing at? Did she *want* me to run away? Has she had enough?" He looks to me for answers I simply do not have.

"Listen, Mike. Your son has been waking me up at 5am all week. It's Christmas Day tomorrow so he's probably going to wake up even earlier. I'm knackered. I'm going to go back up to bed – your bed is mine now - and you can decide where you want to wait for Charlotte whilst you wrap up that present. Hopefully, she'll be back any minute, because Nero is going to be very disappointed if she's not here by the time that he wakes up. His eagerness to see the two of you was the main reason he agreed to go to bed."

Mike's still scratching his head, his face full of confusion.

"Thank you for babysitting, Abi, I know that can't have been easy for you. I'm so sorry, I had no idea she thought I'd run off. I'm really going to pay for this, aren't I?"

"Yep, I think so." I turn to make my way back upstairs.

"Wait!" Mike whispers urgently. I look back. "One more question, why the hell did she think I was in France?"

I shrug.

"Possibly something to do with an ex…?"

His face pales.

"Amélie?" I nod.

"I don't know how you even have an ex considering how long the two of you have been together, but Charlotte seems to think Amélie is your college ex, 'the one that got away', and that you're having an early mid-life crisis. I guess you have a lot of catching up to do, huh?"

"Shit."

"I think you mean 'merde'." I chuckle and head upstairs to bed.

85

I'm a little relieved that my time in charge is coming to an end, I can get back to being irresponsible and selfish. Well, possibly a little less of both, given I have no source of income. What am I going to do?

Stop thinking about it, that's what. Tomorrow is Christmas, I can't worry on Christmas. Even if I am single and jobless. Besides, there's a sexy man waiting for me to reply to his text. Maybe that's what I should do…

19

Christmas Day

Nero holds onto my left hand and I have Jasmine on my right hip as we make our way very slowly down the stairs.

"Do you think Father Kissmas has been?" Nero whispers. I can't stop the image of Jacob slipping into my mind. The man has ruined Father Christmas for me now. He'll never be a friendly old man with a belly in my mind ever again. Not that he ever was. I used to think Father Christmas' were perverts or paedophiles, now I just think of one smoking hot man. A sandwich-stealer with a heart of gold (when he's not hangry). A really nice guy.

I push the thought away as Nero opens the door to the lounge and gasps as he sees all the presents under the tree. At least, that's what I think he's gasping at until I take the final step down the stairs and see for myself.

Tangled up and not appropriately covered, with makeup down her face and his shoulder, are Nero and Jasmine's parents, my sister and brother-in-law. I presume they've made up. I clear my throat as we walk into the room and Nero keeps hold of my hand as if afraid of his scantily clad parents. I clear my throat again,

"We wish you a merry Christmas, we wish you a merry Christmas, we wish you a merry Christmas and a Happy New Year!" I start singing and Nero joins in and then takes over the concert. Next, he belts out 'Silent Night' and then 'Away in a Manger.' This singing alarm clock does the trick and soon his embarrassed audience are sat upright and realigning their clothing.

They have a lovely soppy reunion and begin exchanging presents. There's only one gift for me, a set of smellies from a renowned spa brand. It's not particularly personal, but it's nice enough. We've never been big on presents between us, and if it hadn't been for the Mike's-gone-AWOL fiasco, they probably wouldn't have seen me until the new year. I wouldn't be surprised if this is something Charlotte has regifted to me last minute.

Once all the presents have been unwrapped and Charlotte and Mike have collected all the discarded wrapping paper and started preparing the dinner, I escape to the shower.

Waiting for my straighteners to warm up, I can't help re-reading the message Jacob sent last night. A message I once again ignored because I was scared. He invited me to spend Christmas Day with him. He said, why should we both be alone, when we could be together?

I can't remember the last time I had a boyfriend at Christmas, I usually find myself single by November, early December at the latest. There's something about that time of year that gives guys the ick. It's like they think they'd have to propose, or maybe they just don't want to fork out for a present or risk being forced to spend the day with my sister (it's not like I have a big family). I suppose she is pretty intimidating when she wants to be. Either way, I tend to find myself single for the winter months, and then the dating scene picks up again after Valentine's Day. Men are nothing if not predictable.

Except Jacob. I really thought I had him sussed. That moment at the shopping centre when he jumped the queue and stole my sandwich, I thought he was everything I hated about famous men: arrogant and selfish. And yet, he was just hangry. As was I. And now, knowing what I do about his past and all his charity work… how can I deny that he's a good man? Could he be different to all the others?

I pick up my phone, finally making my mind up. One last try, for the sake of love.

"So, I'll be off then," I announce, feeling refreshed and clasping my rucksack in the doorway of the lounge.

"Don't be silly, you're staying for Christmas Dinner, Abi. You have to after everything you've done for us! We're not kicking you out on Christmas Day!" Mike insists.

"Well, actually, I was invited elsewhere. So, I thought I'd go there…" I reply, studying the keys I'm holding in my hand.

"Would that invite have come from a certain man who likes to dress in red?" Charlotte asks with a teasing tone of voice. Mike throws her a confused look.

"Well…"

"It's Father Kissmas' son isn't it, Auntie?" Nero interrupts, looking proud of himself. Mike's frown deepens.

"Yes actually, it is."

"He smells like popcorn and cheese," Nero informs them before going back to his cars.

"Right. And would Mr Christmas like to come here instead, do you think? I'd really like you to stay," says Charlotte.

"Oh. Well it's a bit soon to be meeting the family, don't you think?"

"He's already met the kids…"

I scowl at her.

"Fine, I'll text him and ask."

There goes my sexual dessert. Seconds later my phone pings.

"He says shall he dress in casual clothes or his Christmas suit? Nero, I think we can let him dress like us today, don't you?"

He isn't listening, he's completely focussed on his new toy car. It's the one Mike picked up from Germany. I guess it really is something special, it's blown the Scalextric out of the competition!

"Say casual, then you can see what he looks like beneath that unattractive suit!" Charlotte giggles and Mike gives her a nudge. I send my reply and then I add with a giggle,

"Oh, I already know what's under that suit. Didn't you watch '*Love Under The Stars*'?"

Charlotte pushes herself upright.

"Oh poo, I forgot he's famous. He's one of those sexy men who went around topless trying to get women to share a tent with him!"

"So, you're dating a man from a reality dating show?" Mike asks, trying to piece the information together. Clearly Charlotte hasn't had time to fill him in yet.

"Long story short, he was our local Father Christmas this year. But yeah, he's off the telly. And, randomly, our dad helped him and his dad out of a tough situation way back. It's kind of spooky, like our paths were destined to cross at some point."

"And he smells like popcorn and cheeeeese!" Nero chirps up again.

"Yes, Nero. And he smells like popcorn and cheese," I verify for Mike.

"Right," he says, nursing a mug of coffee.

"Well, since I'm staying, can I have a coffee?" I start to ask before noticing the look on Charlotte's face.

"No, you cannot. It's cleaning time! Mike, you do the hoovering and I'll get to work on the bathrooms. Abi has probably already told him all sorts of embarrassing things about us, but he can't see our skid marks, I won't allow it! Abi, he hasn't used our toilet before, has he?"

I shake my head, bemused.

"Good. You set up the table and make it look as posh as you can. If there's anything alive and looking pretty in the garden, grab it and shove it in a vase! Okay?"

"Sir yes sir!" I give her a salute.

20

"He's here!!!" Nero alerts the household from his position by the lounge window.

This is worse than inviting a man home to meet my dad. My younger sister and her husband and their annoyingly adorable children are all unreasonably excited and pumped up and wearing their best clothes. Of course, Nero and Jasmine have already met Jacob, but I know Charlotte is going to be assessing whether he's a good match for me and whether he'll be the one to make me settle down. As if it's a bad thing that I'm frequently single and able to drop everything to come to her rescue. Yeah, I bet she hasn't considered that!

My traditional sister believes that if I had a man that was worth my time, a man that cared for me, then my life would be plain sailing; nothing would go wrong, and I would be in a permanent state of bliss. Yeah, right. Because married people never get cheated on or divorced. Or made redundant. Or have husbands seemingly go AWOL due to a lack of communication.

Jacob steps out of his Volkswagen Passat, causing Charlotte's eyebrows to raise almost as high as her hairline, and heads towards the front door, clocking myself and Nero at the lounge window and throwing us a cheeky wink. My heart flutters as I hurry to open the door and let him inside, not really sure how to greet him. I wasn't kidding when I told Charlotte it was early days. I can't deny the spark of attraction that's there, but that's all it is, a spark. It's a long way from a loving relationship, and it started out as a fiery hatred for a sandwich-stealer, let's not forget!

"Jacob, this is my sister Charlotte and her husband, Mike," I make the introductions.

"Ah, the wanderer returns, eh?" he jokes as he shakes Mike's hand.

"Well actually, I never wandered, I just didn't realise my wife had selective hearing…" Mike says carefully, throwing Charlotte a look and biting his lip as if nervous of repercussions. She jokingly swats his arm.

"No calls or texts, this guy sends an email to the address I used at university!" she explains to Jacob.

"No harm done though, eh? I hear you were able to get Nero a special present?"

Mike nods.

"Do you like cars?" he asks. "Let me show you, it's almost as much a present for me as it is Nero!"

They walk off together. I turn to my sister.

"Well? Let's have it!" I encourage her. She smiles.

"So far, so good, sis. He drove himself here in a very standard, non-celebrity style car, he's wearing normal clothes, and he has the body of a god. And, his eyes sparkle. Did you notice that?"

"Not to mention his scent of popcorn and cheese," I add with a smirk.

"Well, I always said you needed more cheese in your life. You're just skin and bones! But honestly, Abi, I think he'll be good for you. Give him a chance, yeah?"

"Why do you say that as if it's my fault that my relationships never last? I'm not the one cheating!"

"I know, I know, you just have really appalling taste in men."

"And you don't think a z-list celebrity who looks like *that* is going to cheat on average me? This is just a festive fling, something to tide him over until his next gig comes along. He's probably going to be the flipping Easter Bunny by spring." We both giggle.

"But seriously, you said he hates kids and yet he helped you more than once. He spent time with all of you. Actions speak louder than words, sweetie," she says wisely.

"Maybe."

"And besides, like you said yourself, it does feel like fate after what our dad did for his dad…"

"I know!" I agree with glee, no longer playing it cool.

*

A few hours later, we push our chairs back from the dining table, stuffed from overeating.

"It's your turn to wash up, Abi, we cooked," says Charlotte.

"As if! I've been cleaning up after your rascals for weeks!" I reply. It's only a minor exaggeration. It was nine very long and very messy days.

"I'll help," offers Jacob. I place my hand on his forearm.

"No, you're a guest," I tell him. "As am I!" I say the words defiantly, turning to face Charlotte. "We'll be having a sit down in the lounge if you need us. Did you bring back any magazines from your travels?"

She rolls her eyes.

"I don't know what you've done to her, Jacob, she never says 'no' to me. But yes, I do have a mag in my bag. I didn't get around to reading it. It's one of those gossipy ones you love. Feel free to take it."

That's all I needed to hear. I leave the table and coerce Jacob to come with me without helping to clear or clean. I've done quite enough for those two, I think. We sit together on the sofa, and I try not to think about how carried away we got the last time we sat here, when he opened up to me and I felt a real connection like I haven't felt in years, or maybe ever.

I open the magazine and lean into him so he can see too. I love these gossip mags, they're my guilty pleasure. I love getting a bit of outfit inspiration with a side of wardrobe malfunctions, and the knowledge that celebrities are people too. They make mistakes like the rest of us, they just have a higher budget and a whole lot more publicity to contend with.

Imagine if it made the cover every time I got dumped or cheated on, it's bad enough having to tell Charlotte. I couldn't cope with millions of people feeling sorry for me.

"Do you think people will write about us?" I ask Jacob. "If you're a Z-lister, does that make me a ZA-lister?"

"I hope not," he sighs. "Things died down pretty quickly after the show. It's amazing how little exposure you can get if you're not chasing it. When the show was on TV every night, but I was back home, I was being followed by paparazzi and questioned by local journalists daily."

"Oh yeah, I always forget it wasn't live. Not that I watched it nightly anyway, I binged it after it finished."

"I think it would have been better if it was played out live. That way I might have missed some of the nasty stuff that was said about me."

"Like what?"

"Rubbish theories about why I wasn't choosing a girl to pair up with in my tent, something about me having back acne, apparently I'm a racist, oh and some woman I've never met sold a story saying she was pregnant with my baby."

"Wow."

"Uhuh, so you can see why I'm not really into magazines like that," he eyes the offending magazine in my hand. Okay, so he has a point, but me not reading it isn't going to stop them writing the stuff, is it?

Before I can do the right thing and put it down, at least until he's gone, a headline catches my eye: **Jacob Chilbeam – Love Under The Sea?** There's an image of him splashing in the sea with a woman in a purple bikini. I look up at him and angle the page his way.

"Oh for F-," he stops himself, "fudge's sake. See! This is what I'm talking about. She's my cousin."

I just look at him as all my fears rush back to the surface. This is what always happens. I'm never good enough. They always leave me because they find someone better. Some blonde bimbo with poker-straight hair and legs that run for miles. My polar opposite. Charlotte might call me skinny because my bum is smaller than hers, but there's no denying the natural curves either side of my small waist, or my sun-kissed skin tone.

Am I just a ploy, a way for him to prove he's not racist? Was all that stuff he told me about his dad and mine even true? Or if it was true, was he using that story to help his agenda? Was it not fate at all? Was I just an easy way to solve a problem, quash a story? Have I totally misread him?

"Abi, please. Listen to me. That's my cousin. You can't believe what you read in gossip magazines," he says calmly.

"But she's so…" I can't finish the sentence as I'm mentally transported back to when I walked in on Toby with our next-door neighbour only a couple of months ago. The image still cuts deep. She was blonde, too.

"Pretty?" Jacob finishes for me. "Yeah, she's a model. We only reconnected a couple of years ago. Her mum is my dad's sister who married a New Zealander when she was twenty, so Carla didn't grow up around here."

"And I'm just supposed to believe you?"

"Well… yeah, kinda. What have I ever done to make you not believe me?"

Be a man.

I can't say that though, can I? Years of failed relationships have taught me that men never stick around, unless they're your father. And then only because your mother ran first. You snooze, you lose.

"I think you should leave," I say quietly.

"Abi, I thought we had something good going here."

"So did I."

"Then don't push me away!" his eyes plead with me.

"I'm sorry, I can't do this at the moment. I need to focus on what's important."

"Love isn't important?"

"Don't give me that! You barely know me. You don't love me, you can't."

97

He leans closer to me, now right in my face. He whispers, "But I could if you let me."

I slap him around the face.

"Shit! Sorry, I just, uh – it was an impulse…"

"Auntie said a bad word!" Nero announces, causing Charlotte and Mike to rejoin us in the lounge, carrying tea towels and wet crockery.

"Well, I guess I'd better get going then," says Jacob. "Thank you both for having me," he tells Charlotte and Mike. "Nero and Jasmine, you, uh, be good." He dips his head in a half-hearted bow, and then makes his way to the door. Finally, he addresses me. "Abi, if you change your mind, you have my number."

The door has barely clicked shut before Charlotte is by my side desperate for answers.

"What the hell happened whilst we were washing up, Abs?"

I point at the photo in the magazine.

"This." Her eyes skim the article. "He said she's his cousin."

"Well, maybe she is."

"When is it ever what they say it is? When Ryan started hanging out at "the golf course" was it really the golf course? No. When I caught Tom having a "business lunch" with an "associate" were they sleeping together? Yes. And let's not forget Toby's affair with THE WOMAN NEXT DOOR!"

"Mmm, yeah, but there are good guys out there too," she says, rubbing my back. "Mike's a good guy."

"I believe he's taken," I joke.

"You know what I mean, maybe Jacob is one of the good ones."

I sigh.

"Father Kissmas' son is a good boyfriend Auntie Abi. You need to make friends with him. Hitting is bad, so you need to say sowee otherwise you'll be on the naughty list." Nero offers his wisdom.

He is kind of right; I shouldn't have hit him. I can't believe I did that. It was like I was hitting every man who ever wronged me, I just had to stop his pretty face from trying to convince me that he's different. How can he be different? Time and time again I end up hurt and alone.

"So, are you going to go after him, or do you want a glass of wine?" Charlotte asks.

"Wine." Always wine.

21

New Year's Eve

I sit beside Dad's gravestone with a beer. He wasn't into flowers when he was alive, so I can't imagine that has changed in death. I've never understood why people buy flowers for the dead, no matter who the person was. Fair enough that some people may have liked flowers, but those who are taken too young, or men like my dad, can't possibly be fussed about people leaving flowers by their gravestones. I'm sure they'd much rather a beer, or a toy, or a bar of chocolate. Not that they'd get to enjoy them, but it's the thought that counts, right?

I crack open the beer and loosen the scarf around my neck. It's homemade and unnecessarily long, handknitted by me over the past few days. I needed something to do that kept my hands busy away from my phone, and my mind off Jacob Chilbeam.

"Hey Dad," I say quietly before taking another swig and deciding to crouch down amongst the icy weeds. "I could really use your advice."

I look around at the other people paying their respects today before we embark on another year without our loved ones. I am the only one here alone.

"Why didn't you tell me about what you did for Jacob and his dad?" I ask the cold grey stone.

"He wasn't one for bragging, your pa, unless it was about you." The voice makes me jump and I drop the bottle of beer and look around. "Sorry, I didn't mean to startle you." He's an older man, probably around the age my dad would have been had he still been with us. He has short grey hair and kind eyes that remind me of someone.

"Sorry, do I know you?"

"Dave Chilbeam. I believe you've met my son?" he holds out his gloved hand. I shake it and then look at the spilt beer beside my feet, the splash marks up his trousers.

"I'm so sorry!" I panic, remembering Jacob's dad was a recovering alcoholic when he met my dad. I look at him as if expecting him to react the way a vampire might to blood.

"It's fine, I'm much better these days. Your dad saw to it that I never fell back off the wagon; he helped me make a life worth fighting for. Do you want to talk about him?"

"Oh, okay. Yes, let's find somewhere to sit, shall we?"

We walk slowly towards a bench at the side of the cemetery. I don't want to rush him; he seems pained.

22

18 Years Earlier

Richard was late to work, again. Breakfast had taken too long after he'd burnt the first round of toast, and then Charlotte hadn't been able to find her lucky socks and he'd had to send Abigail back upstairs to scrub that lip-gloss off before he could finally drop them off at the school gates and head into the office. He wasn't looking forward to seeing his manager as he knew he was already walking on thin ice. He only hoped his situation would allow him to keep his job. The whole office felt sorry for him, the man whose wife had left him and never looked back.

"Richard, glad you could make it. Would you please pop across the road to pick up the coffees for the meeting?" It was a task well below his executive pay grade, but he could hardly say 'no.' He looked up at his manager with a fake smile below his heavy bags.

"Of course, I'll be right back."

The coffee shop was packed full of young professionals with money to spare on expensive coffees. They'd called ahead to make the order, but he still joined the queue as there was no easy way to get to the front and he'd hate to annoy anyone.

The queue moved quickly, and he carefully shuffled forwards behind a young woman wearing stilettos – careful foot placement was key if he wished to keep his toes in good shape.

When he finally emerged from the shop with a cardboard tray of takeaway coffees, he reached into his pocket for some loose change. He liked to give to the homeless because he was afraid that one poor month at work could land him right on the street next to them. He considered it good juju to give when he was barely getting by himself.

His pockets were empty as he stood beside a man and a boy he presumed was the man's son. The man was shaking, possibly an alcoholic, and the boy was thin and around Abigail's age. He should have been at school at this time of day. The boy's eyes pleaded with him and again Richard looked at the father. His arms were folded, fingers digging into thin biceps, as if physically holding himself together. He avoided eye contact and focused on Richard's shoes. There was no smell of alcohol, only desperation, and maybe a little wee.

"Excuse me sir, can you help us?" the young boy asked him.

"I'm really sorry, I don't seem to have any change left," Richard explained, honestly sorry and not just saying it. "Would you like a coffee?"

The boy pulled a disgusted face as his dad reached an arm out and looked up.

"Yes please," said the man. Richard handed him the coffee intended for himself.

"My dad is looking for a job," the boy added.

"What kind of job are you looking for?" Richard asked the man.

"Anything that gets us off the street," he replied. "I used to be an IT Technician, before my life went to shit."

Richard looked from the man to the boy and back again. Maybe he could help these people. Maybe, instead of focusing on his own struggles, he could focus on making someone else's life easier.

"Can you type?"

"Yeah."

"Used a photocopier before? Reasonable telephone manner?"

"Could do," he shrugged, sipping the coffee. Richard needed to get back to work before he got himself into even more trouble, but he hesitated. He wanted to help.

"Look, I can't make any promises, but I might be able to get you a job. It won't be anything exciting, but it'll get you off the street, and you could work your way up. What do you think?"

The man frowned in disbelief.

"Yeah, right. Pull the other one mate. Nobody would hire me."

"I'll lend you a suit and you can wash at my house. I'll ask at work today and then I'll meet you here tomorrow to confirm the details. Okay?"

"Seriously?" the man asked, stunned.

"Yes."

"But why would you help me?"

"Because I've been down on my luck too. My wife left me with two daughters to raise on my own and I'm barely scraping by. If it weren't for the kindness of my colleagues,

104

I'd be right there next to you. So, I'm playing my luck forward."

"Okay," the man said, clearly still sceptical. Richard started to walk away and then stopped and turned back.

"What's your name? For your job application."

"Dave. Sorry, David Chilbeam."

"Alright Dave, I'll see you tomorrow. And you, keep your dad safe, okay?" Richard looked at the young lad with the weight of the world on his shoulders.

"Thank you, mister."

They watched the kind man walk away.

23

18 Years Earlier: The Next Afternoon

"I can't believe it!" said Dave, unable to contain his grin. "They hired me! Jake, they hired me!"

"Yes, Dad! I knew you could do it!" Young Jacob jumped up and gave him a fist bump. Richard couldn't help but smile at their pleasure, he was happy to help.

"I think we should go out and celebrate, don't you?" he asked them both. The boy's eyes opened so wide that Richard suspected they hadn't been out to celebrate anything in a very long time.

"Oh no, that's okay, you've done more than enough. We'll be out of the shelter in a month!" said Dave.

"Honestly, it's my treat. You deserve to celebrate, today is the first day of the rest of your lives!" Richard insisted, barely glancing at his watch. He had places to be, but he'd make time for this.

"Ah, well, if you insist. But nothing fancy, like. I'm sure Jake would like a burger, wouldn't you?"

"Yes please!"

A burger was something Richard could afford to buy them, and it had the added benefit of being served in a place without an alcohol licence. He hadn't asked Dave if he was sober, but he was certain that it was his daily battle. He hoped that with a little trust, he would be able to help keep the man on the right path.

The three of them sat and ate burgers and fries with chocolate milkshakes, and Richard felt happy that he had truly helped them. And he planned to continue to help them, at least until they were living comfortably. He would put good karma out into the world in the hope that it would be returned someday; be that to him, or to his daughters when they need it.

When they finished eating, Richard opened his wallet to give them some cash to buy some more clothes and bits, and a photo of his daughters, Abigail and Charlotte, fell out. They were dressed up in pretty dresses for a wedding. He caught the young boy looking at it before he could tuck it back away.

"They're my daughters," he said, answering the boy's unspoken question. "I've got to go now, they're in a dance show tonight. My eldest is in Grade 5 Ballet. Maybe you'll get to meet them someday."

24

"And the rest, as they say, is history," Dave says, straightening up and looking at me with a familiar twinkle in his eye. "If it weren't for your dad and my son, I wouldn't be here today." I nod. "Listen, I don't know what happened between you and Jake, but I do know two things," he holds up two fingers. "One, my son is a good man and I'm not just saying that because I'm his dad; and two, he really likes you. He called me after he took you ice skating, and I could hear it in his voice. He's never spoken like that about anyone, so you must be pretty special. Being Rich's daughter, I'm confident that you are. I know it's none of my business, but if there's anything I can do to help you to work things out, please let me know. I owe your dad my life."

"Well," I say, considering this opportunity. "I'm not sure if it will help as I have my own issues to deal with, but you could corroborate his story…"

"Okay, tell me. I'll see what I can do," his fingers trace his moustache. I hesitate, pondering how much of a difference his answer will make. Have I already made up my mind regardless, or am I willing to give Jacob another chance?

"Do you have a sister?"

"Yes," he answers with a frown.

"One that married a man from New Zealand and moved over there?" He nods.

"Yes, Sally."

"And does Sally have a daughter who is now a renowned international model called Carla?"

"Ah," he smiles. "I know what this is about."

"You do?"

"I collect everything to do with my boy, I'm so proud of how far he has come with so little help from me. Your dad nudged him in the right direction, offering him internships and the like, but I was no role model. These days I keep every newspaper and magazine article, good and bad, to remind myself of the reason I stopped drinking. I wanted Jake to have a good life, and he does. No matter what they say, he has enough money, and he's a good man. That's all I ever wanted."

"So, you've seen the article with him on the beach with Carla?"

"Yes."

"And you can confirm that she's his cousin?"

"She certainly is. It came as a surprise to me too though, I guess she takes after her dad in the looks department because my sister wasn't anything special."

I release a sigh of relief. Jacob was telling the truth. Well, that, or his dad's a big fat liar too.

"So, what else is holding you back?" Dave asks me.

"History, I suppose. A truckload of bad relationships. I just don't want to be hurt again." He nods with understanding.

"Do you know what a wise man once told me? Every day is a chance to start writing a new story. Blank page, clean slate; you know what I mean? Every day when you wake up, you can choose to close the book of the past, of your mistakes or the things which haunt you, and you can open a new book and start again: page 1. If you had never had those bad relationships before and this was a brand-new book, would you still be dating my son?"

A small smile creeps across my face.

"Then I think you know what you need to do."

25

But it's not that simple! I can't just text him and be like "sorry, I was wrong." I need to show him, and I need to be sure. I need to see him in the flesh, surprise him. I need to test fate. Which is why, on New Year's Eve, I find myself walking arm-in-arm with my sister towards a charity striptease. I think you can guess who the star of the show is.

"Can we sip cocktails whilst they seduce us with their snake hips?" Charlotte giggles, wobbling in her heels.

"Yes, but the moment you start trying to touch them, I'm cutting you off! You're a married woman!"

"Boo!" she laughs again as we approach the entrance and prepare to show our tickets and have our bags checked.

We must have been lucky to get tickets so last minute because it is packed inside. I scan the room but of course there's no sign of Jacob. He's probably backstage getting ready.

We make our way to the bar before finding our seats, to placate Charlotte. She hasn't had a night out in a very long time, and it shows. I think she's reached her drinking limit already whereas I still feel painfully sober (and nervous).

I'm not quite sure what to expect from coming here. Jacob may spot me in the crowd watching him, but will he think it's a coincidence, or will he know that I came for him? Will he invite me up to the stage? Will he come and find us afterwards? Why didn't I just send him a text?

I gulp my Sex On The Beach and wait.

"You need to relax," says Charlotte, dancing in her seat.

"I'm trying!"

A group of women stumble into their seats in the row behind us chatting loudly,

"He's so fit, isn't he? I can't believe he's single. Do you think he'll see us back here? I have no idea why no one picked him on *Love Under The Stars*!" It takes all of my self-control not to turn around and claim him as my own.

By the time the show starts, my drink is long gone, and I am so nervous I feel sick. The men do their thing, dancing and stripping to music, their bodies greased to accentuate their muscles. There is no sign of Jacob, the star of the show.

Do I even want to see him like that? Even if it is for charity, I don't know if I'll be able to get over him showing off his body to all these other women. I want to be the only one who gets to see him, touch him; I don't want to share. I want him to be mine.

I shout into Charlotte's ear that I need the toilet and then squeeze past the rest of the people in our row. I make my way down the centre aisle, out through the reception area and towards the exit on my mission to wait outside where I can breathe without watching gyrating men.

"I'm sorry but I can't do it!" I hear a man's voice in the corridor, out of sight.

"What do you mean, you can't do it? We are talking about twenty-five thousand pounds, Jake. Get your kit off and

112

your charity gets twenty-five grand. What's there to think about?"

"My self-esteem? My dignity? I'm not a piece of meat!" I stop and listen.

"That didn't bother you on '*Love Under The Stars*', did it?"

"Maybe I learnt my lesson!"

"Maybe you aren't the charity ambassador I thought you were!"

"Maybe I don't care what you think! I'm done. You're fired. I'm leaving!"

"You can't just leave; we signed a contract!"

"Watch me!"

Before I can move out of the way, Jacob storms round the corner shirtless and shiny and holding a t-shirt to his chest as a short but large man with a very pink face follows behind. He stops dead and the man nearly crashes right into him.

"Abi?"

I smile awkwardly.

"I, er, came to see you."

"Well, the show's off," he snaps, stretching his t-shirt over his head and covering himself up. I quickly reach into my bag, open the secret pocket, and pull out the contraband I hid from security. A bag of toffee popcorn.

"Peace offering?" I say, holding it out. "I didn't come to see the show, I came to see you. To apologise."

"Alright," he says, taking the bag. "Paul, call me a cab," he orders the man I assume is his manager. "We'll be waiting outside."

"But Jake, I really think you ought to come inside. It's five minutes, for twenty-five grand!"

113

"Last chance, man." Jacob warns before pouring the popcorn into his mouth. The man hesitates, seemingly weighing up the pros and cons of fighting Jacob on his decision.

"I just don't want you to miss out on this opportunity. This is big money!"

"Wrong answer." Jacob throws the empty popcorn bag into the bin and grabs my hand, leading me outside. We start walking down the street in silence, Jacob almost pulling me along with his fast pace. We don't stop until we reach a late-night café.

"Do you mind?" he asks.

"Not at all, I'm starving," I admit. I'd been too nervous to eat properly earlier. We head inside and order two cheese toasties, then sit in a booth whilst we wait for them to be brought over to us.

"So, you wanted to see me," he states bluntly, his anger at his manager still bubbling under the surface.

"Yes," I answer, my chin held high.

"Did you change your mind?"

That familiar sparkle in his eye returns.

"Maybe. I met your dad." He frowns, and the sparkle disappears.

"You did?"

"Well, I went to see mine, at the cemetery, and he was there."

"Huh."

Our toasties arrive, but they're too hot to eat.

"So, what did he say?"

"That you're a great man and that he thinks you really like me. And he corroborated your story about your cousin,

114

and what happened with my dad…" Jacob nods and wipes his fingers on a napkin.

"I think I need to tell you something."

"Okay," I look him in the eye, my heart ready to hurt. Does he not want me after all? Have I got it all wrong?

"The reason I'm not myself tonight, isn't because I'm hangry and I didn't want to get my kit off for charity. It's because," he looks down at his toastie and pulls off a corner, then sort of studies it rather than eating it. He puts it back on his plate and then brushes his fingers off again. "My Dad died this afternoon."

"What? But… but I just saw him this morning! He seemed fine. How did he? I mean, what happened?" I reach out for his hands, holding them for reassurance. I want to comfort him. I know what he must be going through.

"He knew he was dying; it wasn't a shock. He was saying his goodbyes, even to those who had already gone." He bites his lip.

"Like my dad." I finish for him. I continue to hold his hands and study his pained expression. "Do you mind if I hug you?"

"I can't think of anything I want more."

We move to the side of the table to stand up and hold each other. The café is empty except for a couple of staff, most people having better things to do on New Year's Eve.

I pull away a little to face him but keep hold of his arms.

"I know it's bad timing, but I really want to kiss you."

"I really want to kiss you too," he replies with watery eyes. Fireworks set off by someone too impatient to wait until midnight light up the sky outside as we kiss like nothing else matters.

26

"So, does this mean we're official?" I ask as we arrive at Jacob's remarkably average apartment.

"Do you want to be my girlfriend?" he answers my question with another question, but I'm not letting him off the hook that easily.

"Do you want to be my boyfriend?"

"I want to be so much more than that, but I'll settle for boyfriend for tonight," he grins before kissing me again. His kisses are so addictive, I never want to stop.

"Look, it's nearly midnight!" I say, bringing our attention back to the TV.

"Are you ready to start the next chapter of our lives with me?" he asks seriously.

"Why yes, I think I am."

"I'm going to need more than a 'think' ma'am," he teases me.

"Alright, yes, I am. I pick you, Jacob Chilbeam. Can I please go back to your tent now?" I raise my eyebrows in what I hope is a suggestive way.

"If by 'tent' you mean, 'under my covers naked,' then absolutely," he winks.

"Hmm, what about your Father Christmas hat?" I joke.

"I don't know, have you been a good girl this year?"

As Big Ben hits midnight in London, Jacob carries me through to his bedroom and I forget all about the hat.

THE END

Please let me know if you would be interested in reading a sequel focused on Charlotte's adventures as she scours France and the UK for her missing husband, with travel disruption, in-laws, and ex-girlfriends to contend with!

(I'll get it ready for Christmas 2024!)

Drop me a message on social media or mention it in your review.

Acknowledgements

My biggest thanks must always go to my mum, my biggest supporter, who is always there for me despite how much she is struggling herself.

To Andrew and Daisy, the couple who inspire me the most and are never too shy to like or share my posts on social media. Thank you, and I'll see you lovebirds at Christmas!

To Dad, again, it's not your kind of book, but thank you for taking the time to support me and give this a read (she writes, confident in the knowledge that you will!)

To Marti, you probably don't realise how much help you were to me recently just by being there and listening. You're a great friend and supporter and I will never forget that.

To my Facebook fans, particularly: Stacie, Sara, June, Teresa, Anne, and Barb, you are consistent likers and commenters, and I want to give you extra thanks! Please keep doing what you're doing, it all helps! (And if anyone else feels like they should be on this list, keep up the good work for a mention in my next book!)

Finally, and perhaps most importantly, I thank **you**. You probably had no idea what I was going through when I wrote this story, but by reading it (and reading it all the way to the acknowledgements, no less) you are cementing my decision to never back down (again), to put myself first, and to fight for what I believe in (including myself).

For now, my romantic heroes may all be fictional, but I've yet to find a better escape than inside a book. I hope my festive rom com made you smile and feel warm inside, whatever your situation.

Thank you for reading.

Chloë xx

About the Author

Chloë is one of us.

She's that girl who reads on her lunchbreak, on the train, at the hairdressers; that girl who has bags under her eyes because 'one more chapter' rolled on and on until the book was finished at 3am, on a work night.

Chloë is also a writer and, until February 2022, she kept that pretty quiet. She hid her 'true' passion beneath her love of other people's books, by studying English and American Literature at University, and only ever talking about what she was reading, not what she was writing.

From a very young age Chloë filled notebooks with stories and now she's grabbing that childhood dream of becoming an author with both hands.

'Christmas Wishes & Popcorn Kisses' is her fourth book, with lots more planned for the future.

ALSO BY CHLOË L BLYTH

THE DANGERS OF DREAMING
FANTASY ROMANCE TRILOGY

WHAT IF YOU WEREN'T THE ONLY ONE WATCHING YOUR DREAMS?

ELLA survives on a steady diet of frozen pizzas, white wine, and rom coms. Her love life is akin to a magician's vanishing act, and her only friend is a work colleague. But she's fine, she's...
okay.

Loneliness is a state of mind Ella refuses to acknowledge. And why should she? When she closes her eyes, she's never alone. She's with him, her dream man. A man she is literally dating in her dreams.

ADAM knows it's not right; he knows it's forbidden, but what choice does he have? He has to know her. He longs to feel her gaze, to be the object of her affection, to hear her laugh up close, to squeeze her hand and hold her tight; to comfort her when she cries.

He's not obsessed, he's just in love with someone he can never have. Adam is a stickler for the rules, and it is simply not permitted. He'd never put Ella in danger, not on purpose anyway.

But life doesn't always go according to plan.

~

'Duplicity' is the first instalment of a new action-packed fantasy romance series 'The Dangers of Dreaming.' In this world, dreams are no longer private and dream manipulation runs rife.

When you close your eyes, you don't shut out the bad guys, **you let them in**.

Find out more and buy the complete trilogy now on Amazon!

FOLLOW ON

Instagram and Facebook
@chloeblythauthor

WEBSITE

https://chloeblythauthor.com

If you enjoyed this book, please post a review online to help other readers discover this new festive rom com!

Even a few kind words will make a difference.

Thank you!

Printed in Great Britain
by Amazon